The Moirai's Gambit

Forged in the Fires of Fate

IMMANUEL RAJALINGAM

PREFACE

Every journey begins with a spark, a moment that shapes the path ahead. The Moirai's Gambit: Forged in the Fires of Fate is not just a story about fate, friendship, and resilience—it's a reflection of the incredible people who have been my guiding light along the way. This novel is a tribute to my family, whose love and support have been the foundation of everything I do. You have been my strength in times of doubt and my compass when I've felt lost. Every page of this book carries a piece of you, a testament to the unwavering belief you've had in me.

To my friends, who have walked beside me through every storm and triumph, this story is also yours. The characters, their struggles, their victories—are all inspired by the moments we've shared. You've taught me the value of loyalty, the power of laughter, and the importance of standing tall, even when the odds are against you. For that, I am forever grateful. I owe a special thanks to Kaviya and Sarah. Your motivation and encouragement helped me unlock the potential of this story when I couldn't see it for myself. You pushed me to dive deeper, to trust in the journey, and to bring this novel to life.

Without you, The Moirai's Gambit would have remained just an idea, not the fully realized tale it is today. Lastly, a heartfelt thanks to Rakesh Johnson and Manikandan, whose creativity and vision shaped the stunning cover that draws readers into the world of this novel.

Your work captures the essence of this story, reflecting the battle between fate and choice, and I'm deeply honored by your contribution. The Moirai's Gambit: Forged in the Fires of Fate is a story about choices, destiny, and the bonds that shape who we become. It's about the risks we take and the challenges we face, not alone, but with those who stand by us when it matters most. This book is for all of you—for the love, support, and belief that helped forge my own path through the fires of life.

Thank you, from the bottom of my heart.

Welcome to The Moirai's Gambit—where fate's hand is never far, but true strength lies in how we choose to play the game.

CONTENTS

Chapter I

Family is the Heart of a Home.

Are you familiar with the Goddess of Fate? If not, let me explain. I am the Goddess of Fate, known as Moirai, one of the most powerful Greek gods ever. I am the one who decides an individual's fate or destiny, and I control the threads of life, while you are nothing but the dolls in my hands.

Most people in the world have families, whether good or bad; family is the best habitat for humans. Similarly, I have a family; I have two sisters: Clotho, the youngest, who is the goddess of a nine-month pregnancy; Lachesis (Me), who measures the thread of life for every human being using a measuring rod; and Atropos, also known as the cutter of the thread of life or the reaper. Our father is Olympus, the chief of the gods, and you can call him Zeus, the powerful god of the entire universe. Even our other brothers and relatives fear him. We the Moirai sisters have the exceptional ability to act on our own. My mother's name is Themis, also known as the goddess of divine law or the goddess of justice.

Among all of Zeus's wives, my mother, Themis, holds a special place in his heart. They seem to be made for each other. This is my beautiful family, and we live happily in a heaven you have never known. Based on my experiences dealing with the fates of millions of lives, I will narrate the story of one poor soul who lives in Tamil Nadu, India. Though the Tamil culture differs from our Greek culture, the Tamil language and culture are ancient and still in use by its people, which intrigues me.

The man's name is Irvin, now twenty-three years old. His father's name is Rajan, a retired government officer, and his mother's name is Maanya, a typical Indian housewife. He also has a brother, Shane, who is three years older than Irvin, but they look like twins and act more like friends than brothers, much like my sisters and I.

Maanya is a devout Christian who prays to God in the early morning and attends church meetings without fail. Her ultimate goal is to raise her sons to be good Christians. Rajan, the head of the family, was born and raised in a rural area, and through hard work, he became an assistant account officer. Unlike other Indian fathers, he is different, including my own father. Typically, fathers are more authoritarian, and children are afraid of them.

However, Rajan never laid a hand on his sons in his lifetime. He was a passionate father who spoke openly to his sons. Irvin's friends were amazed and became fans of him. Therefore, Irvin and his brother, Shane, never hesitated to speak to their father. Unfortunately, this couple faced numerous challenges in their early years. For instance, three years after their marriage, Maanya gave birth to their first child, who tragically died after just three or four days due to health issues, despite resembling Rajan.

According to the Bible verse, "Pursue, for you shall surely overtake them and without fail recover all," after this tragedy, Maanya gave birth to their second child, Shane, and three years later, Irvin was born. However, tragedy struck again when, on Irvin's 29th day, he was diagnosed with a rare disease called septicemia, with a low chance of survival.

Maanya fervently prayed for her child's survival, as did the church, while Rajan cried profusely, and little Shane was left in Maanya's mother's care. Maanya played a vital role, solemnly promising God that she would never wear jewelry for the rest of her life if her child survived. This demonstrates a mother's love for her child, sacrificing the wearing of jewelry, which is not easy for any woman.

Despite Rajan's opposition to this decision, they made it for the sake of their child.

Personally, I am amazed by her decision; I could not make such a bold decision myself. Sometimes, I am proud to be a goddess instead of a mortal. This is the birth history of Irvin. Irvin began fighting for his survival from childhood, which is why I personally chose to narrate his story.

Chapter II
The Shifting Sands of Innocence

Irvin and Shane are very spiritual and memorize Bible verses without fail. Shane is a brilliant student who consistently earns first prizes in academics as well as in Sunday school. Sunday school is where children are taught about the Holy Bible, and tests are conducted to foster their spiritual growth. Christians often divide their lives into two aspects: worldly life and spiritual life. Maanya places importance on spiritual life while also considering education. Therefore, Shane has consistently achieved the top rank in every academic year, whereas poor Irvin has received average marks in academics and has typically ranked second or third in Sunday school.

Irvin has been a playful guy from childhood until now. He never concentrates on his studies, focusing instead on games with the neighborhood boys and girls. Sometimes, Shane invites Irvin to play cricket with his friends. Since Irvin didn't know how to play cricket at that time, Shane's friends would have him pick up the ball from the boundary line. When Irvin was in third grade, he became friends with a Muslim boy named Asiq.

Usually, school starts at 9 a.m. and ends at 3:50 p.m., but Maanya is busy with her church activities, so she enrolled them in tuition for an extra hour. Most Indian schools have this tuition system for weaker students, so Asiq and Irvin always sat on the bench together. During this time, they had a clash over which religion is superior: Christianity or Islam, Lord Jesus Christ or Allah. Irvin won this clash, and Asiq came to believe that Lord Jesus was the true God.

But after two days, Asiq's mother went to Irvin's house and quarreled with Maanya. It was only then that Maanya learned about the incident. She apologized for her son's behavior and reprimanded Irvin. I know this incident is controversial, but it is still a story. This serves as an example of how devout Irvin and Shane are to their religion. Irvin's family moved from another place called Kettapettai. This is where Irvin lost his innocence.

When Irvin came to this new place, he didn't know anybody, and neither did his family. The place felt strange to them, and Irvin and Shane missed their old friends. Shane and Irvin felt lost in this unfamiliar environment.

However, after a few days, Shane started to play with the neighbor's kids, who were about the same age as him. Irvin was the youngest boy in the group, so he used to play with the girls, engaging in games like hide and seek and other indoor activities, while Shane and his friends played cricket. This was when Irvin met Mani Varma for the first time. Although Shane and Mani Varma were the same age, Mani Varma spent most of his time with Irvin.

After school, Irvin and Mani Varma would ride their bicycles to hang out every day. Mani Varma taught Irvin everything he knew: how to fly a kite, how to tie the thread for an effective kite experience, and how to apply Manja (a mixture of various materials with ground glass pieces applied to the thread to cut others' kite threads). Initially, Irvin didn't eat street food, especially fried chicken feet, but Irvin and Shane got used to it because of Mani.

Everyone has a negative side, and for Mani, it's his habit of hankering untidily and spicing up his stories with lies, also known as "put-up stories," to bolster his image. Initially, Irvin and his friends believed his tales, but eventually, they discovered the falsehoods and began to mock Mani. However, their love for him remained steadfast, exemplifying how male friendships operate. Despite their flaws, they accept one another and enjoy life together. Irvin, being a keen observer, absorbs everything and learns from it. One day Mani introduced two friends, Paraman and Pawan, to Irvin, he didn't anticipate that they would eventually split into two groups.

Life is like a BP monitor, full of ups and downs. While studying in the tenth grade, a huge storm came toward Irvin. Jada, Shane's best friend, complained to their parents about Paraman and Pawan, accusing them of being bad guys who tease Shetty, their neighbor girl. Jada and Shetty were childhood friends, but as Jada reached adolescence, his feelings changed and he developed a crush on Shetty. Pawan appeared smarter to Jada, and she began to create a bond with him. Jada felt possessive of Pawan and decided to drive both Pawan and Paraman away from the area by falsely reporting them to his parents.

Jada's parents and other neighbors also agreed with their sentiments, particularly against Irvin's new friends, especially Mani, Paraman, and Pawan. So, Jada's parents and the other neighbors argued, "Maanya doesn't allow those boys into your house, and they are bad guys. You must reprimand your kids to end their friendship."

However, Maanya disagreed with them, asserting, "This is my house, so I have to decide whom I allow or not.

Additionally, I have two sons, so their friends come to our house, and I can't accept your theory." Despite Maanya's explanation, the neighbors didn't compromise. They reported the issue to Irvin's house owner and suggested that Rajan's family be evicted. However, Maanya clarified this matter with her house owner. Irvin's neighbors refused to compromise at all; they were determined to force Irvin's family out at any cost.

After this issue, the friends' groups split into two: Jada with the neighbor kids, and Irvin with Shane, Mani Varma, Paraman, and Pawan. Initially, Irvin's circle seemed small, but after a few months, it expanded significantly. During the evening, ten or fifteen members would gather at Irvin's house or on the corner of the street to chit-chat. Irvin learned many things from his friends; for instance, Pawan was the first in their group to have a Chinese mobile phone, which sparked Irvin's interest in technology. Paraman taught him how to ride a motorbike, as well as techniques for fighting and easily defeating opponents. Paraman also introduced many friends from various places to Irvin, expanding his social circle. Whatever the situation,

Paraman always stood by Irvin's side, acting as a shield for him.

One day, Mani encouraged Irvin to mock Jada, so Irvin began relentlessly teasing him wherever Jada went. Initially, Jada reported Irvin's actions to Shane. Then, in a second instance, Jada said, "Tell Irvin to keep quiet. I am older than him, so I can't tolerate this. If it happens again, your brother will face severe consequences." Shane warned Irvin about Jada's complaint, but Irvin didn't take it seriously due to Mani's influence.

The next day, Irvin began mocking Jada again, this time with Mani. However, Jada responded by slapping Irvin, leaving Mani shocked. Irvin felt helpless, especially since his own brother supported Jada. Overwhelmed, Irvin cried a lot, and Mani reported the incident to Paraman. Unable to tolerate this disrespect, Paraman and his group planned to retaliate against Jada.

However, Shane informed Jada about Paraman's plan, prompting Jada to seek refuge at his aunt's house. Interestingly, Jada's aunt happened to be Irvin's former tuition teacher. She summoned Irvin to meet her and facilitated a peace treaty between Irvin and Jada.

Had she not intervened, it's likely that Paraman and Irvin would have seriously harmed Jada. If Shane had intervened, he would have faced the same fate. From Paraman, Irvin learned that a true friend supports their friends, whether the situation is good or bad, no matter the cost.

From that day onwards, Irvin began to admire Paraman. Through Paraman, Irvin learned the art of humility and helping others. Maanya developed a positive perspective about Paraman, and Irvin gained a good reputation within Paraman's family as well. Following this, Irvin expanded his circle of friends, forming a diverse group with varying ages, resembling a gang. For instance, if Irvin was 15 years old, his friends might be 18, 19, or even 24. Irvin admired his friends' attitudes and gradually lost his innocence.

Chapter III
A Tale of Two Groups and One Street

After the separation, Jada's group remained smaller while Irvin's group grew larger. Many of the new boys introduced to Irvin from various places used Irvin's house as a hub. After school, college, and work, they would gather at Irvin's house. Initially, Rajan didn't approve of these gatherings, but over time, he grew accustomed to them and even felt proud, boasting about it to his sisters and relatives. Jada's group and Irvin's group avoided each other entirely, not even exchanging greetings when they crossed paths.

Naren acted as a mediator between the two groups, but only when it came to playing cricket, not for any other interactions. This conflict persisted for three years. Naren, being significantly older, was six years senior to Irvin. Although Naren usually supported Jada's group, he eventually realized that the feud was pointless and started to broker a compromise between the two groups. However, this wasn't their genuine reason for seeking a compromise. During this period, the Saurashtra family constructed their house in Kettapettai and relocated there. Who are the Saurashtra? Allow me to explain.

The Saurashtra is a community from Gujarat whose members speak Gujarati, not Hindi. Many centuries ago, they migrated and settled in the southern part of India. First impressions are crucial, so the Saurashtra family made an effort to establish a good reputation. They invited Irvin to their house, served him two dosas, and spoke kindly to Mani Varma and Naren.

However, one day they revealed their true colors. The two groups used to play cricket in the street, often referred to as gully cricket. The Saurashtra family disliked this because they felt disturbed by the noise. Interestingly, they would close all the windows and doors to watch Hindi serials, so it was puzzling how the outside noise bothered them. Naren pondered the situation deeply and concluded that the best solution was to unite the two split groups into one. Not only Naren, but Jada's family also opposed the irrational behavior of the Saurashtra family.

The cricket bat and six stumps were kept in Irvin's house, but one day, Saurashtra Aunty noticed them and entered Irvin's house without any greeting. She stole their bat and three stumps and ran back to her house. Maanya and Irvin were shocked by her ill-mannered behavior. Irvin reported the incident to his friends, and they tried to devise a plan to recover their cricket equipment from her. Fortunately, around nine p.m., Kavin encountered Mani and Irvin, and they informed him about the incident.

At first, Kavin spoke politely to her in an attempt to retrieve the cricket kit, but his politeness was ineffective. He then switched to a more assertive approach and threatened her to return the kit. Frightened, she handed the cricket kit back to Irvin. However, the Saurashtra family harbored a grudge against Irvin's family. They were considered a curse on Irvin's street.

After this family moved to the street, many problems arose. They began to differentiate between tenants and landlords, with the landlords viewing tenants as inferior. Consequently, they all turned against Irvin and his family. Rajan was only vaguely aware of this because he was always busy with work. Irvin and his friends couldn't tolerate this nonsense, so they started causing trouble for the Saurashtra family.

So Irvin and his friends indirectly targeted the Saurashtra family by placing rotten eggs and tomatoes in front of their house. On another occasion, they urinated at their front gate at midnight to avoid being caught. Another day, Irvin and his friends gathered on Irvin's terrace. Mani collected 10 bucks from his friends and bought fried chicken feet. They consumed the meat, and all the bones ended up on Saurashtra's terrace. The next morning, the Saurashtra uncle and his son cleaned up the bones left by Irvin and his friends.

Chapter IV

Irvin's Gang

From Crackers to Gears

Diwali is one of the most celebrated festivals in India, and people of various religions enjoy it by bursting crackers. It holds a special significance for them. They pool together funds from everyone to purchase crackers and traditional attire like shirts and veshtis (sometimes influenced by the black shirts and white veshtis seen in the Malayalam movie "Premam"). In Tamil Nadu, there are two types of crackers used: branded crackers and local crackers, known as "Naatu Vedi" in Tamil.

Mani Varma prefers local crackers because since childhood, he and his brothers have been accustomed to using them. Compared to branded crackers, local ones are more powerful and effective, often utilizing more paper for a louder BOOM sound. However, Irvin lacked experience in this area. Despite this, he asked his father Rajan for two thousand rupees to buy a cracker.

They took a motorbike and travelled nearly 9 kilometres to purchase crackers. Irvin and his friends gathered various types of crackers such as Golden Vedi, Mappalai Vedi, Sky Crackers, Yaanai Vedi, etc. They lit the crackers in front of Irvin's house and captured all the festivities on Paraman's iPhone. But after the arrival of the Saurashtra family, that aunt filled a bucket with water and poured it on the floor or sometimes on the crackers, preventing Irvin and his friends from lighting them. If Diwali came, there would be a conflict between the boys and the entire family. She shouted at Irvin to burst the crackers in front of their own house.

Even during festive times, she caused trouble for Irvin's family. Unable to tolerate this harassment, Irvin and his friends threw crackers (Gold Vedi) into the Saurashtra house. During this phase, Irvin and his gang began to evolve in transportation. Their friendship started on bicycles and progressed to XL Super, which have no gears and only 45cc engines. These bikes did not belong to them; they belonged to their fathers. In Kettapettai, they became known as the "XL Boys" because they roamed the streets riding XL Super. Interestingly, they also had a WhatsApp group named "Roadside Roamers," known as தெருபொறுக்கிகள் in Tamil.

Paraman knows how to ride a motorbike (with gears), so he teaches Irvin to ride one as well. On the other hand, Pawan joined Polytechnic College, so his father Ramesh bought a Dio scooter for him. The name "XL Boys" gradually faded away. Meanwhile, Mani bought an RX Z.

In the meantime, Irvin's XL became useless, so Maanya had a plan to buy a second-hand motorbike. During that time, Irvin used to ride fast in the streets, which led many people to complain to Maanya. Moreover, Irvin was inexperienced with gear bikes, prompting her to consider purchasing a second-hand bike. At that time, Irvin had a desire to buy the RX-100, an antique two-stroke motorbike by Yamaha.

Irvin planned to deceive Maanya and purchase the RX-100, but the plan was foiled by a second-hand dealer who warned, "This vehicle is designed for high speeds, so it could be dangerous for Irvin." Naturally, Maanya rejected the RX-100, and Shane opted to buy the Pulsar 135 instead. As for Paraman, he doesn't own a bike of his own, but he occasionally rides his father's bike or his brother Paari's bike.

Paari is not originally from Kettapettai, but he frequently visits his grandma's house and has a strong bond with Irvin. Despite not excelling in academics, Paari showed aptitude in business. After completing his schooling, he took over his father's quarry business. Irvin rarely watches movies in theaters, but he was permitted by Rajan later on. Maanya disliked this decision. Irvin is an ardent fan of Thalapathy Vijay. However, obtaining tickets for FDFS (First-day First-show) is challenging because tickets are often sold at inflated prices. Sometimes, Vijay's fan clubs control the FDFS tickets, selling them privately to club members.

Paari had connections and managed to purchase the tickets at regular prices, allowing Irvin and his friends to spend less and enjoy the FDFS like everyone else. Within this group, each member had distinct roles and purposes that evolved over time.

Chapter V

Irvin vs Saurashtra

A Tale of Resilience

In the meantime, Irvin's neighbors organized all the landlords and formed an association for the street, with Saurashtra being a member of this association. One day, Keshava and Ahsan were playing badminton on the street, right between Irvin's and Saurashtra's houses. As they began their game, Saurashtra Aunty suddenly became furious and started quarrelling with Ahsan and Keshava, using abusive language.

Ahsan remained quiet, but Keshava couldn't tolerate her language. He shouted back, giving her a taste of her own medicine, also using abusive language. This escalated the situation further. Keshava left the scene on his R15 bike, returning after thirty minutes with Sharon and Aamir. They summoned the entire family to the street. Keshava vented all his pent-up frustration against Saurashtra's family, confronting them with repeated use of abusive language.

Saurashtra uncle attempted to assault Keshava, but Keshava wasn't afraid of him. Instead, he stood firm with a racket in hand and said, "What are you hitting me for? Motherfucker!! If you have the courage, go ahead and hit me." Selvam was intimidated by this statement and never stepped out of his building. Keshava's family and relatives gathered at the scene, along with other people from the street. Unexpectedly, Paraman and his brother Paari entered the scene and tried to mediate. However, Saurashtra Aunty scolded Paraman using abusive language. Paari became agitated and intervened, threatening Saurashtra uncle.

Paari said, "Nee epadi di en thambiya ketta varthai la thittalam. Dai potta paiyala nee veliyavaa da gommala unmela en lorry vittuyethurae nee epadi uyiroda iruka nu paakurae" (How could you speak to my brother so disrespectfully? You good-for-nothing, you're still alive? I should have run you over with my truck, you idiot.)

Paraman pulled Paari aside and urged him to leave the place. Meanwhile, Irvin was in the restroom, and Rajan and Shane were asleep. The commotion from the fight woke them up, and Irvin soon joined to witness what was happening. The association leader called all the members and instructed them to gather at Saurashtra's house.

However, there was a twist: the altercation was between Keshava and Saurashtra, but the association leader and the majority of the members were accusing Irvin's family in front of everyone.

Rajan listened to everything quietly, while Irvin couldn't tolerate the accusation. He shouted at his dad, "What's going on, Pa? The fight is between them! Neither Shane nor I were involved in the scene. Why are they blaming us? This isn't fair! I can't take this nonsense anymore. I'm going to get involved in this mess." Rajan replied firmly, "Hold on your ass now! Stand by me, alright son? Today, we need to remain silent and watch the show. "Irvin obeyed his father's words. Many people had gathered there, so Keshava's family and relatives pulled him away, and later all of them dispersed from the place. But this was just the beginning. After that, Irvin and his friends would face many problems they had never anticipated.

During birthdays, as usual, ten to fifteen members gather in front of Irvin's house to celebrate. Sometimes, Mani removes his silencer and revs the engine loudly, creating a significant noise. Paari joins him with his customized Royal Enfield silencer, adding to the bike's roar. They also give birthday presents in the form of playful birthday bumps.

Birthday bumps refer to a tradition where friends playfully tease the birthday person by throwing items like eggs, sometimes even rotten eggs, or concocting mixtures like Parotta gravy (Salna) with added color powder or Cow dung in flour, as happened on Irvin's birthday. They mash this mixture on the birthday boy's head and then take selfies to post as stories on Instagram. This is seen as a display of camaraderie among men, but such moments don't always endure.

During Paraman's birthday, Irvin and his friends planned a midnight celebration. Paraman arrived at Irvin's house accompanied by Velu. However, some of Irvin's friends were accustomed to drinking alcohol and smoking, which caused discord within the group. Therefore, the birthday boy had to either give money or buy liquor for his friends who indulged in such activities. They also treated the friends who abstained from alcohol. Irvin and some his friends adhered to certain principles beyond those found in religious texts. Their foremost rule was "under no circumstances, no matter what, never touch alcohol or cigars."

So Velu, intoxicated, attends Paraman's birthday celebration. At midnight, Keshava bursts a cracker, leading to a significant incident. Keshava's tenant who had recently returned from abroad, arrives and shouts at Irvin and his friends. Due to Velu's intoxication, he attempts to attack the foreign returnee and threatens his life. This incident brings disgrace upon the foreign returnee and prompts him to seek revenge. Unfortunately, Irvin's family is caught up in this tragedy.

Afterwards, Irvin instructed his friends to flee, and Keshava left on his own without informing Irvin. The foreign returnee is affiliated with an Islamic political party, so he brings three party members along with a police officer. Irvin is fearful of the police and hides on the terrace, but Shane bravely confronts the police officer, party members, and the foreign returnee. During this confrontation, Shane mentions his preparation for the UPSC examination, which prompts the foreign returnee to threaten Shane with legal action.

Rajan was genuinely frightened by this incident, and he apologized to the police officer on behalf of his son, considering his son's future. On the other hand, Saurashtra and the association leader gathered all the members to witness this incident. It was the first time Irvin and Shane received a black mark due to Keshava's actions. Following this incident, the Saurashtra family obtained the police contact number from the foreign returnee, viewing it as a potent tool to intimidate Irvin and his friends.

This incident brought about a drastic change in Irvin and his friends' lives. They could no longer celebrate birthdays on the streets; if the Saurashtra family spotted a cake box, they would call the police station, resulting in two police officers coming to inquire and warn them. Therefore, Irvin's friends decided not to bother Irvin anymore, so they stopped gathering at Irvin's house and frequently changed their meeting places.

During the COVID-19 pandemic, the world descended into chaos. Initially, the Indian government closed schools and colleges. As the COVID-19 outbreak intensified, the government imposed curfews and quarantine measures, urging people to stay at home and venture out only for emergencies or essential needs.

Irvin and his friends couldn't bear staying inside their homes and felt very bored. They decided to organize a friendly tournament using the Carrom board game. In the evening, more than ten members gathered on Irvin's home terrace, played Tamil songs on small speakers, and enjoyed the tournament.

However, Saurashtra came to know about this and called to complain about Irvin and his friends. After a few minutes, police officers arrived at Irvin's house, honking their horns and shouting, "Hey! Everybody get down!" Upon hearing this, Irvin peered from the terrace and saw two police officers on the ground floor. Shocked, Irvin warned, "Hey, it's the police! Everybody run!" Some of his friends jumped from the backside of the terrace and successfully escaped.

But Irvin, Shane, Paraman, Jaya Krishnan, Paari, and Robin remained on the terrace. Paari, being the larger guy, attempted to hide behind an opened slab. Despite the seriousness of the situation, they all made fun of his attempt to hide. Soon, police officers arrived on the terrace and instructed them to kneel down on the floor.

However, none of them complied. Paari started arguing with the police officers. Even though it was a hilarious moment, Irvin and his other friends couldn't laugh at the situation and they released Paari. At the same time,

Robin's father arrived; being a member of a political party, he managed to secure Robin's release as well, requesting leniency from the police. The officers considered his request and advised them to play indoors with no more than four persons at a time.

Irvin questioned the statement, asking, "Sir? Can we then play Carrom with four members?" The home-guard retorted, "Hey, I will chop off your dick, idiot." Following this, Irvin and his friends gathered at Raviteja's house and played a friendly game of rummy in his storeroom. This is how they passed their time together with family and friends.

In Irvin's life, he enjoyed a lot during his childhood but also faced many challenges as he matured. In India, if the police come searching or arrive at their homes, it's detrimental to their future. Typically, such incidents involve rowdies and criminals, but Irvin and his friends are just students who play in the street. Irvin's family are tenants and opposed to their neighbour's ideologies, which led neighbours to make several attempts to drive them away. However, they forgot about God. We stand for justice and will protect Irvin, his friends, and his family no matter what!

Chapter VI

Irvin

From Ancestral Soil to School Halls and Life of Contrasts

I am the Goddess of Moirai, also known as the God of Fate. I guide individuals toward their destinies. In previous chapters, I recounted the joys and sorrows experienced by Irvin, his friends, and his family, detailing how they faced their tragedies. Now, let us delve into Irvin's origins and his academic days.

In this modern era, almost everyone attends school to receive an education, which helps develop their knowledge and cognitive abilities, essential for surviving in a competitive world. School education plays a vital role in everyone's lives. However, some people drop out of school to work for daily wages.

There are various reasons for dropping out, such as being unable to cope with the demands of education or family poverty preventing them from continuing their studies. According to the latest National Survey of India, the country's literacy rate in 2022 was 77.7%. While this percentage is significant today, it took several decades for India to achieve this level of literacy. With that introduction, let me narrate the story of Irvin's origins.

Rajan and Maanya were both born in Kadapapalayam, but Maanya's father was a headmaster and her mother a schoolteacher. Due to her parents' professions and frequent transfer orders, Maanya's family often moved and eventually settled in Thendralpalli. On the other hand, Rajan was born into a farming family; his parents were knowledgeable only about farming, and he was raised in Kadapapalayam along with his four siblings. Through his hard work, Rajan studied well and secured a government job.

In Tamil tradition, when a bride gets married, she moves to her groom's house. So, Rajan and Maanya got married, and Maanya moved to Kadapapalayam with her beloved husband Rajan. After three years, Maanya became pregnant and gave birth to their first son, but tragically, the baby died and was buried in the house Maanya's father had built. Two years later, Maanya became pregnant again and gave birth to their second son, Shane, who was born in Kadapapalayam.

Shane looked like Maanya, with her fair skin tone, nose, and hair. In essence, Shane was the male version of Maanya. When Maanya became pregnant for the third time, both Rajan and Maanya hoped for a baby girl. However, fate (Me) had other plans, and Maanya gave birth to our protagonist, their third son, in Thenralpalli. Rajan and Maanya were unsure what to name their child, so Maanya sought advice from a pastor's wife, who suggested the name Irvin. Irvin resembled his father Rajan, with the same dark skin tone, hair, and eye colour. Consequently, the locals nicknamed him Rajan Jr

Initially, Rajan worked as a junior assistant, essentially a clerk. This was a turning point for Rajan's family. Typically, the government issues transfer orders to its employees, and Rajan received such an order. Maanya, accustomed to living in Kadapapalayam, was reluctant to move to another district. However, Rajan believed that moving to Thendralpalli would benefit Shane and Irvin's education. Finally, Rajan received the transfer order to Thendralpalli. At that time, Shane was 2 years old, and Irvin was an infant.

Rajan and his family moved to Thendralpalli and settled near Maanya's parents' house. When Shane turned three, Rajan and Maanya began searching for a school to enroll him in. After a few days of deliberation, they decided on St. Tiny Flower Matriculation Higher Secondary School in Kettapettai. Founded in 1977, this school is known for providing excellent education at a reasonable cost. Despite being a government employee, Rajan's position only provided a modest income, making Tiny Flower School an ideal choice for their children's education.

Unlike many children, when Shane first joined the school, he never cried due to the new environment or being separated from his parents for five hours. However, Shane, being a quiet, calm, and brilliant boy, soon adapted and enjoyed his time at school, performing well academically.

Meanwhile, Irvin didn't start speaking until the age of three. During those times, children were typically admitted to Lower Kindergarten (LKG) at age three. Thus, Rajan and Maanya enrolled Irvin in school at the age of four. Surprisingly, Irvin showed no fear of school and was indifferent to other children's cries. While Shane balanced his playtime and study time well, Irvin struggled with maintaining this balance and often neglected his studies. Shane excelled in all subjects, whereas Irvin barely passed all subjects.

Rajan didn't pay much attention to Shane and Irvin's grades due to being a workaholic; he often left for the office at nine in the morning and returned home at ten or even midnight. He believed his role was to ensure they had the means for education, while he entrusted Maanya with their academic progress.

Consequently, Maanya was content with Shane's academic performance but concerned with Irvin's inconsistent results. She became strict with Irvin, pressuring him to improve his grades. Whenever Irvin gets distracted, Maanya forcefully knocks on his head, sometimes causing his head to spin and occasionally swelling due to her strong hand.

In the next examination, Shane, as usual, achieved very good marks in all subjects. Surprisingly, Irvin also performed well and obtained good marks across all subjects. This success helped Maanya recognize Irvin's potential and playful nature. In the beginning stages of Irvin's life, he is quiet, disciplined, and obedient to his parents and teachers.

Even though he is friendly by nature, when he becomes angry, he never lets the person responsible go without hitting them. This becomes a habit early on for

Irvin. In kindergarten, Vicky, the class leader, tries to bully him. Irvin cannot tolerate this and, in a fit of anger, repeatedly scratches Vicky's face with his sharp nails. Irvin's class teacher reports the incident to both Vicky's and Irvin's parents, requesting a meeting with them.

The next day, Vicky's parents and Maanya have a heated argument. Vicky's parents express their concern over their son's suffering, while Maanya justifies her son's behavior. Finally, Irvin's class teacher concludes that both Irvin and Vicky made mistakes. As a result, she removes Vicky from his leadership position and gives Irvin a warning.

At age three, Irvin was unable to speak fluently in Tamil. Maanya understood him through his hand gestures and broken Tamil. When Irvin wanted to drink tea, he asked Maanya for a cup. Maanya said, "Irvin, wait, son. I will give you the tea after it cools down." However, Irvin misunderstood and thought she was refusing to give him tea. While Maanya was cooling the tea, Irvin picked up a lightweight stool and tried to hit her from behind.

Every human has a good and bad side. Likewise, Irvin loves to spread love and happiness wherever he is present, and with his charm and way of speaking, he creates bonds of friendship with others. These are some of the positive aspects of Irvin. However, on the negative side, Irvin cannot control his anger. If someone offends or hurts him, he reacts violently and often holds a grudge forever.

Chapter VII

Threads of Fate

Irvin, Jothika, and the Changing Tides

At the age of eight, Irvin's family migrated to Kettapettai. After a few months, Shane invited his friend Gokul and introduced him to Maanya and Irvin. Meanwhile, Irvin, Shane, Jetta, and Shetty all attended tuition at a nearby house. The tutor's name was Rekha. She had one elder sister and one younger sister, but compared to her siblings, Rekha was a gorgeous woman, so Irvin often gazed at and admired her.

Shane suggested that Gokul join Rekha's tuition center, and Gokul told his parents about it. Gokul's parents agreed to send him to Rekha's tuition center, but there was a catch: Gokul mentioned that Shane was also a student there. Knowing Shane's reputation as a brilliant first-rank student, Gokul's parents were convinced. Gokul was mischievous, so they also decided to send their daughter to Rekha's tuition center.

Gokul's sister's name is Jothika. Gokul and Shane are classmates and friends, while Jothika and Irvin are grade mates, meaning they are both in third grade but in different sections. Irvin is in Third 'B', and Jothika is in Third 'E'. Gokul introduces Jothika to Irvin. Jothika is surprised to learn that Irvin is Shane's brother because this is not their first meeting.

Let me explain the flashback behind Jothika's shock. One academic year ago, Irvin and Jothika were both in second grade, but Jothika was in 'E' and Irvin was in 'B'. During that time, there was a shortage of teachers at St. Tiny Flower School, so one teacher handled all the subjects except for P.T. (Physical Training) classes. One day, Irvin's class teacher resigned from her job due to her upcoming marriage.

Due to the lack of teachers, there are no substitute options available. St. Tiny Flower School divides its school into two sections: primary and secondary. The primary section comprises grades LKG to Third grade, with students transferring to the main school for higher grades. Additionally, St. Tiny Flower School is governed by nuns, totalling four nuns—two for the primary section and two for the higher secondary section.

Therefore, the nuns in charge of the primary section decided to finalize the separation of the second grade 'B' students from their class roll numbers and temporarily shuffle them into other sections. Irvin and his friends thought it was going to be tough because they were separated by roll numbers, which were assigned alphabetically. However, fate (ME) had other plans. Irvin was sent to the 'E' section and stayed there for a whole week, while the students of the 'B' section suffered due to lack of space. Each section had approximately 50 to 55 students. The students of the 'B' section had to sit on the floor, while the students of their respective classes sat on benches.

This made the 'B' students uncomfortable. During the P.T. period, Irvin was alone because his friends were in different sections, so he sat in a corner by the pillar, passively observing. At that moment, Jothika noticed Irvin sitting sadly under the pillar and invited him to join her and her friends in playing. Irvin is an ambivert, so initially, he hesitated to join in, but after Jothika invited him several times, Irvin agreed to play with them.

Jothika likes how Irvin plays and speaks, but there wasn't enough time to spend together to form a bond because the administration appointed a new class teacher for Irvin's class the following week. Irvin, along with his friends and classmates, returned to their original class. However, Irvin is unaware that this incident will have a significant impact on his life.

Currently, Jothika is shocked when she sees Irvin, but Irvin doesn't remember her face. Jothika's family is interested in sports activities as well. Gokul is very well trained in cricket, and Jothika herself practices karate, so she knows how to defend herself. On the other hand, Shane is average at cricket, and Irvin is inexperienced in fighting.

Chapter VIII

The Dance of Trust and Treachery.

Irvin and Jothika encountered one another at Rekha's tuition center. Irvin believed it was their first meeting, but Jothika remembered him. They soon became best friends, spending a lot of time together at tuition and often playing games at Jothika's house. Jothika also formed friendships with other tuition students, but she became particularly close with Shetty, Alia, and Irvin. When Rekha declared a holiday from tuition, Gokul and Jothika would visit Irvin's house, where Irvin, Shetty, Alia, and Jothika would play and socialize. Meanwhile, Shane, Gokul, Jetta, and the older kids would go play cricket.

In contrast, at school, Irvin and Jothika act very differently. They do not speak to each other; they just exchange smiles and move on. Jothika and Irvin like each other but don't show it because of their shyness. Jothika discusses Irvin with her closest friends, Akila, Christy, Logini, Swathi, and Phoebe. Irvin similarly mentions Jothika to his friends, but they don't take it seriously.

In his childhood, Irvin was the craziest fan of Thalapathy Vijay, a top actor in Tamil Nadu. He admired Vijay and often imitated him, copying his mannerisms and actions from movies. During interval time, Irvin would perform stunts like chasing his friends to impress Jothika. Meanwhile, Jothika and her friends would laugh at him, tease Jothika, and nickname Irvin "the scene" because of his show-off behavior. Whenever they saw Irvin, they would chorus his nickname. Irvin, lacking the courage to face them, would run off to his classroom.

Shetty doesn't like the friendship between Irvin and Jothika, so she devises a plan to separate them. Shetty begins to plant seeds of doubt in Jothika's mind, suggesting that she and Irvin are in love. Being very young, Jothika feels awkward and starts believing what Shetty says. Meanwhile, Shetty tells Irvin that Jothika speaks badly about him, which makes him angry with her. Shetty successfully achieves her goal and eagerly waits to see the fallout. This creates a conflict between Irvin and Jothika.

After the tuition session, Gokul and Shane usually talk about their own things, and Irvin and Jothika do the same. During tuition, Jothika smiles at Irvin, but he doesn't respond, which hurts her feelings. After the session, Jothika angrily approaches Irvin and demands, "Why are you ignoring me?" This question sparks a major conflict. In her anger, Jothika slaps Irvin on the left cheek. Confused for a moment, Irvin then retaliates by kicking her in the stomach. Shetty quietly observes the scene, but Gokul and Shane suddenly intervene, stopping the fight. Gokul then takes Jothika home.

This incident frequently runs through Jothika's mind, causing her to become afraid of Irvin. As a result, Jothika refuses to go to school and develops a high fever. Meanwhile, Irvin feels remorseful about the incident and looks for Jothika at school but can't find her. The next day, Gokul confides in Shane, explaining his sister's fear of Irvin and her love for him.

Gokul requests that Irvin should no longer see Jothika, and Shane relays this message to Irvin, who agrees to the request. Thus, the beautiful saga of Irvin and Jothika ends like ashes from burning paper. After a few days, Irvin and Jothika return to their normal routines, but Jothika's friends Logini, Swathi, and Phoebe still tease Irvin whenever they see him.

Apart from Irvin and Jothika's situation, Irvin and his friends thoroughly enjoyed their time at school. Being super seniors to the lower-class students, they felt a sense of superiority. In the third grade, Irvin achieved the third rank, which earned him the teachers' favor, especially from the Tamil teacher who had converted to Christianity and joined Irvin's church. As a result, Irvin was spared from heavy punishment, allowing him and his friends to have as much fun as they wanted. They ran across the floors and sometimes ragged the first graders. Irvin and his friends believed that no one could control them, so they engaged in many mischiefs in the primary school.

One day, Irvin discovered that Shetty was the main culprit behind his issues with Jothika. Although he felt extreme anger toward Shetty, he hesitated to reopen the issue and decided to let it be. However, Irvin began to feel ashamed of himself for trusting Shetty more than Jothika. This intense anger towards Shetty turned into a grudge in Irvin's heart, and he waited for the perfect opportunity to seek revenge. To Irvin, Shetty was nothing more than a Puke (despicable) human being.

Chapter IX
Ink and Reflections

After Irvin and Jothika separated, Irvin was promoted to fourth grade and moved to the main Secondary School. This was his first time at the main school, where the buildings were much larger and older than those at the primary school. Additionally, there were four P.E. teachers instead of just one. Most importantly, the rules were different and more stringent compared to those at the primary school. Irvin struggled to adapt to the new rules and teachers.

Many things changed in Irvin's usual routine, but Phoebe and her friends never stopped teasing him. The school organized the classrooms in a row, with fourth grades A to F all on the first floor. During breaks, Irvin never stayed in the classroom. Instead, he and his friends spent their breaks chatting in the corridor, fighting in the boys' restroom, or watching their seniors fight.

On the other side, Phoebe and her friends came out for their break. Since they shared the same corridor, they saw Irvin with his friends and started calling him by his nickname, "Scene," before moving on. However, Jothika was missing from Phoebe's group. Irvin became frustrated because he couldn't enjoy his school life like he did in primary school, so he went to school without any enthusiasm.

One day, Maanya told Irvin about Shane's academic malpractice. Shane had forged Rajan's signature on his report card because he scored lower than usual. While recounting Shane's story, she used the abbreviation "sign" for signature. Unfortunately, Irvin misunderstood Maanya and firmly remembered Shane's malpractice actions. Due to his lack of interest in school, Irvin left his English fair notebook incomplete. The English teacher announced the submission date, and on that day, she marked the notebooks with a red ink pen, which was also called a "sign." Irvin, remembering Shane's malpractice as described by his mother, misunderstood the meaning of the word "sign."

At school, the term "sign" refers to the teacher checking and marking students' notebooks with their signature. However, Shane forged Rajan's signature on the report card, so Irvin had the misguided idea of imitating his English teacher's signature. After school, Irvin got money from Maanya, bought red ink from the stationery store, and began signing his unfinished chapters.

Many Indian films portray English and science teachers as beautiful, kind, and alluring angels, objectifying women in unrealistic ways. In reality, they are quite different. In Irvin's case, his English teacher is dark-skinned, overweight, strict, married, and has two kids. (Disclaimer: I'm not objectifying any women in the above paragraph. I am merely highlighting the difference between expectations and reality).

The submission day arrived, and the students stood in line for her signature. Irvin saw that some of his friends and classmates were being severely punished by her for not completing their fair notebooks. Her slaps sounded like loud crackers echoing in the classroom.

Irvin was horrified, imagining what would happen if she discovered his mischief. When the English teacher called Irvin's bench mates to get her signature, he stood last in line, his heartbeat increasing as the queue shortened. Finally, Irvin showed her the finished chapter. She ticked the pages and placed her iconic signature on the last page. Irvin began to breathe a little easier, but his English teacher had a small doubt. She turned the pages backwards and discovered Irvin's forgery.

Already tense, his English teacher transformed into an angry Kali Amman with her long steel ruler. She grabbed Irvin's shirt with one hand and continuously beat him with the other, scolding him for what he had done. Simultaneously, she slapped him on both cheeks. This went on for several minutes until the steel ruler bent. Suddenly, the bell rang, signaling the end of her period.

Irvin temporarily escaped, but she demanded to meet his parents the next day. If he failed to bring them, he would be sent to the principal, worsening his misery. Irvin felt ashamed for the first time because she beat him in front of his female classmates.

Irvin had no other option but to bring his parents. After school, he confessed everything to Maanya. Irvin expected her to become furious and scold him, but instead, she was saddened by his behavior. This broke Irvin's heart because he had never seen his mother like that before. The next day, Maanya and Irvin went to school to meet his English teacher.

Maanya waited a long time to see her, and finally, she appeared. They talked and discussed Irvin's behavior, and the English teacher warned him about his actions. Irvin had a habit of learning from his mistakes and not repeating them. After this incident, he diligently completed all his work, finished all his fair notebooks, and successfully completed his fourth and fifth grades.

Chapter X

Whispers of Affection

A Journey of Friendship and Revelation

Irvin was promoted to the sixth grade and has slowly adapted to the school norms. He is now interested in his studies and has gained a bit of confidence due to two reasons. First, at Tiny Little Flower School, boys are required to wear trousers from lower kindergarten to fifth grade, but from sixth to twelfth grade, they can wear pants.

Irvin loves wearing pants rather than trousers. Second, at that time, the Tamil Nadu government mandated that all matriculation schools follow a unified set of textbooks under the scheme called "Samacheer Kalvi." Compared to the matriculation syllabus, Samacheer Kalvi was easier. These two changes motivated Irvin to go to school.

At that time, the school management decided to shuffle the students' sections and posted the new class lists on the notice board. Irvin and his friends were anxious about the changes, and while some of them were moved to other classes, Irvin remained in the 'B' section.

Because of this announcement, Rajan dropped Shane and Irvin off at school early. Irvin chose the last bench, placed his bag on the desk, and went to see his former 'B' section classmates. Later, when Irvin returned to his classroom, he discovered that Jeya Krishnan and Rashad Khan had been shuffled from the 'E' section to the 'B' section. Irvin already knew them from lower kindergarten, but Jeya Krishnan was from the 'E' section, and Rashad Khan was from the 'C' section.

These three knew each other but weren't in close contact until they later became part of Irvin's group at Kettapettai. Irvin entered the classroom during prayer time, and everyone was present. He recognized some faces, but others were new to him. At that time, Irvin's class had sixty-four students. During prayer time, all the students closed their eyes and recited the school's iconic prayer, but Irvin kept his eyes open and observed the others.

Meanwhile, Irvin's instinct tells him that "someone on the second bench from the girl's side is watching you." Irvin is surprised to see that Phoebe and Logini are present in the classroom, and Phoebe is staring at him intently. At first, Irvin is frightened to talk to Phoebe because, for the past three years, she had teased him continuously.

However, later on, Irvin and Phoebe got to know each other and became friends. On the other side, Keshava introduces his friends Amir Raja and Reviteja. Amir teaches Irvin Tamil bad words in English, like "flower + in + tie = to" which translates to a Tamil bad word. Irvin used these equated bad words with his classmates, and soon this "equation" spread like wildfire.

Nizim is a favorite student of Irvin's class teacher because she was his teacher in fifth grade 'F' and is now his class teacher again. Nizim and some girls who dislike Irvin reported the equation to the class teacher. The class teacher became furious because she thought Irvin was a good Christian boy and had a good reputation. This equation incident began to tarnish that reputation.

The next day, during the first period, she calls Irvin out and asks him about the equation. Irvin is shocked to learn how the equation got leaked to his class teacher. During this inquiry, Irvin's detractors shout his faults to the class teacher, causing her to become even more furious. She beats him with a wooden scale and forces him to kneel down and pray for his sins in front of all sixty students.

Irvin feels deeply ashamed, especially since he was embarrassed in front of Phoebe. He feels very bad about himself and begins to target Nazim to seek revenge.

Irvin skillfully maintains his path of revenge while also building friendships with other students. Thanks to his charm and sense of humor, the girls in his class surround him during breaks, laughing at his mannerisms, slang, and jokes. Meanwhile, Irvin and his friends plan to confront Nazim. Although Nazim speaks bad words more fluently than others, some of his female supporters help him escape from the teachers.

Irvin decides to gain the friendship of the class girls and then exact his revenge. Irvin and his friends corner Nazim in the boys' restroom and beat him up inside. But later, Nazim and Irvin became best friends. Everything went as Irvin had planned. However, in the same timeline, Irvin and Phoebe frequently stared and mocked each other. They had a different kind of feeling rather than friendship but didn't show it. In Irvin's classroom, his friend Samar proposed to Rizwana, and she accepted. This became a hot topic in the classroom, but the students refused to report it to the class teacher.

One day, Naomi confesses to Irvin and his friends, saying, "I love Cain, Samar loves Rizwana, and you love Phoebe." Irvin and Pugalarasan are surprised and ask, "How do you know about this?" Irvin then asks Naomi directly, "How did you know that I love Phoebe?" This question surprises Naomi because she had just made an assumption and didn't actually know that Irvin loved Phoebe.

This excites Naomi, and she feels compelled to tell her friend Phoebe. However, Irvin asks her not to reveal it to Phoebe just yet. Naomi agrees not to disclose Irvin's feelings to Phoebe, but she and Irvin have a secret conversation about Phoebe's behavior. Irvin assigns Naomi the task of impressing Phoebe. However, Naomi struggles to keep it hidden for long.

Phoebe becomes suspicious about Irvin and Naomi's secret conversation, so she continuously presses Naomi for details. Unable to handle the pressure, Naomi reveals the truth: "Irvin loves you, and I'm helping him." From that day onwards, Phoebe starts caring about Irvin, but she stops talking with him. She doesn't refuse or accept his proposal; instead, she asks him to wait for her reply. This situation continues until the annual examinations.

Naomi hurriedly came to Irvin with the news that Phoebe wanted to see him. Irvin and his friends were suddenly excited upon hearing this and they went to meet Phoebe. When Phoebe saw Irvin, she approached him and they shook hands. Irvin couldn't help but wonder what was happening. Along with the handshake, Phoebe gave Irvin a tiny Bible verse stand with a letter. Irvin was so excited, thinking it might be a love letter.

However, when he opened it at home, he was surprised to find it was just a collection of riddles. Now the annual vacation begins.

Chapter XI
Whispers of Allegiance

Many of the students commute to school by bicycle, and Irvin knows all the types and brands because he is a member of the Junior Red Cross (JRC) club. The scouts and JRC members arrange the bicycles in neat rows and maintain the parking area. Irvin sometimes uses his brother's bicycle, occasionally borrowing Rajan's XL Super Bike. Maanya and Irvin decide to buy a new bicycle and plan to tell Rajan the following week. Rajan and Irvin then go to town and purchase a brand-new bicycle. Irvin loves his new bicycle because it has advanced features compared to Shane's. Thus, last year, Irvin rode his bicycle to school every day.

Phoebe's father works as a bank manager, so he is frequently transferred to different locations. He spends time with the family only on government holidays. Consequently, Phoebe comes to school with her mother and sister. Phoebe's mother is a homemaker who always wears makeup and never steps outside without it.

After vacation, Irvin and Shane are promoted to grades VII and XI, respectively. Irvin is eagerly waiting to see Phoebe, the girl he admires. Usually, Irvin arrives at school at the last minute, but after falling in love with Phoebe, he comes to school as early as possible to admire her beauty. Phoebe wears earrings that complement her uniform perfectly. She styles her hair to the side, which looks beautiful, and her long hair impresses Irvin, especially because Maanya also has long hair. Although Phoebe often keeps Irvin waiting for a response, she frequently looks at him and teases him.

At this age, Irvin underwent a character change. He admired Nizam's ways and understood that only two types of students garnered attention and fame among peers and teachers. The first type of student excels academically, achieving high marks and earning the admiration of both teachers and students, which then spreads throughout the school. The second type is an average or underperforming student who gains notoriety through mischief and rule-breaking, making their name infamous.

Irvin had the potential to score high marks but didn't put in the effort. Therefore, he chose the second path. Irvin intentionally involved himself in trouble, often coming to school without completing his homework, especially in math. Through his friendship with Nizam, Irvin gained a notorious reputation among teachers and students. Despite the negative attention, Irvin began to feel proud of his actions.

While standing outside due to punishment, Irvin and Nizam would often watch volleyball matches from the second floor or Irvin would lean against the door and admire Phoebe's beauty. As planned, Irvin's name spread throughout the school. Meanwhile, Irvin's teachers discussed how to report his behavior to his parents and discovered that Irvin is Shane's younger brother, which shocked everyone because Irvin was the complete opposite of Shane. Shane was a quiet, diligent student who went home right after school and never engaged in any misconduct. Teachers respected Shane and often praised him to Maanya during parent-teacher meetings.

The teachers decided to report Irvin's behavior to Shane and ask him to convey this information to Maanya, but this approach failed. Meanwhile, Irvin waited for Phoebe's response for nine months. Frustrated by the lack of response, he eventually approached Naomi.

Why has she taken so long to respond to my proposal? I can't wait any longer. I'm asking her one last time: will she accept my proposal or not? If she says no, I will never interfere in her life again. Naomi delivered Irvin's message to Phoebe. Thirty minutes later, Naomi returned to Irvin and said, "Phoebe is ready to accept your proposal."

From that moment on, they began to exchange their emotions through their eyes or via messages delivered by Naomi. Irvin's friends also voluntarily supported his love life. However, some of their classmates became suspicious of Phoebe and Irvin's relationship. One classmate, a tattletale, reported their love story to the class teacher. When the teacher came to question Irvin, he skillfully handled her inquiries.

Irvin was very happy with his love life, and his attendance improved because of it. One day, the school management announced that, in celebration of Children's Day, students were allowed to come to school in colorful attire with some restrictions. It had been a long time since the management had made such a decision, so the students were very excited. Irvin was especially excited to see Phoebe in colourful clothes.

The next day, all the students arrived in colourful attire. Irvin wore a green shirt, black pants, and black shoes. Rashed Khan wore a pair of soccer boots that his father sent from abroad, unaware that they were meant for playing soccer, not casual wear. When Irvin saw Phoebe in colourful clothes for the first time, he admired every inch of her tremendous beauty. She had her long hair in a single braid, and wore a red churidar with long sleeves, miniature red dice earrings, red sandals, and red glasses. Irvin couldn't take his eyes off her.

After lunch, the school management decided to show the Tamil movie "Thanga Mengal" in the smart class. Students sat with their best friends to enjoy the show. Samar, Phoebe, and Rashed Khan became benchmates due to a punishment for Rashed and Samar. Seizing the opportunity, Samar moved to sit with Irvin's friends in the last two benches. Samar, Pugalarasan, Nizam, and Irvin's other friends encouraged Irvin to sit with Phoebe to watch the movie.

Initially, Irvin blushed and hesitated, but his friends persisted and encouraged him to sit in the corner of Phoebe's bench. Irvin eventually accepted and took the corner spot next to Rashed Khan, Phoebe, and two other classmates. Naomi understood the situation and encouraged Phoebe for this gesture. As Irvin settled in, Samar hurriedly moved to the second bench and pushed Irvin inside.

Samar asked Rashed Khan to come outside, but Rashed refused. Irvin gained confidence and then asked Rashed Khan to move aside. Khan stepped down from the bench and sat in the corner. Now, Irvin and Phoebe sat together, watching their very first movie in school.

But this incident led to chaos in the classroom. Once again, the troublemaker of the class reported this incident to the class teacher. This time, Irvin's teacher confronted Irvin about his love life. The next day, the teacher entered the class furiously and began to question Irvin about the previous day's events.

Initially, Irvin denied the accusations against him. The teacher became even angrier and struck him with a wooden ruler, which broke into pieces. She then decided to borrow a steel ruler from the next class and continued to strike him. She also questioned Jeya Krishnan and Naomi about delivering Irvin's messages to Phoebe.

Jeya Krishnan accepted the accusation willingly, as a reward for helping Irvin, he received punishment with the steel ruler. Despite being lean, Jeya Krishnan happily endured the pain for his best friend Irvin, whom Irvin greatly admired. Naomi escaped punishment by telling the truth. The class teacher then questioned Phoebe in the corridor, where they had a conversation before returning to the class. The teacher said, "Admit your mistakes, or else you will be punished for the entire period."

While the class teacher was called to the staff room for some reason, Irvin's friends moved from their bench to the first bench. Pugalrasan suggested that Irvin should admit his guilt and avoid going to the principal's office. This was because a few days earlier, Pugalrasan had been questioned by the teacher about his feelings for Logini. He admitted it and was let off with a warning. When the class teacher returned to the classroom, Irvin finally admitted his guilt. She scolded him harshly and warned him before leaving.

Irvin was shocked at how the class teacher knew about the Children's Day incident and his messages. He decided to investigate to find the culprit responsible. Irvin began questioning Naomi and other friends who were close to him. Most of them claimed not to know who the culprit was. Irvin grew suspicious of Anitha because she seemed uncomfortable and shouted at Irvin during the show. He tasked Saaib with confronting Anitha.

Saaib, known for bringing the tastiest non-vegetarian food to school, had his food snatched and half of it eaten by Irvin and his friends. Despite this, he remained loyal to Irvin due to his popularity and large circle of friends. Saaib was eager to join their group.

Within a few weeks, Saaib uncovered the whole truth and identified the black sheep of the classroom. He relayed the truth to Irvin: Anitha was the one who complained about Irvin, Phoebe, Jeya Krishnan, and Naomi. Upon learning the truth, Irvin exploded in anger and confronted Anitha.

He demanded to know why she had been causing trouble. What was her motive? Anitha revealed that she had liked Irvin since childhood but was upset that he had fallen in love with Phoebe. Feeling possessive, she wanted Irvin to herself and thus reported him and Phoebe to the class teacher. Irvin was furious at her confession. He wanted to hit her but couldn't because of her gender, so instead, he cursed at her, made her cry, and forced her to leave.

Chapter XII
Rebellion of Hearts

After Anitha's irrational behaviour, Irvin and Phoebe temporarily separated for their own well-being, yet they never stopped gazing at each other. Though they couldn't express their love in words, they communicated it through their eyes, creating an enchanting connection. Beyond the romantic aspect, Irvin became a renowned student among the teachers. The teachers often conversed about Shane being virtuous and Irvin being mischievous. Irvin and his friends took control of the class, with Irvin himself acting as the class leader. In this manner, he successfully completed the seventh grade.

After the vacation, Irvin and his friends are promoted to the eighth grade, but the school administration asks the students to revisit last year's classroom. The school management decided to convert the school from a co-educational institution to a convent. Irvin and Pugalarasan were shocked by this news, while some students were pleased. Last year, numerous incidents occurred that the school management couldn't control, especially those involving the twelfth-grade students. Ajith, Rajesh, and

Mugesh, who were in the computer science group, rode high-speed motorcycles to school without licenses. Ajith was infatuated with Punitha, but unfortunately, this situation reached their parents, causing significant turmoil. These incidents created a negative reputation for the school.

During the vacation, the school teachers and administration discussed and decided to transform the school into a convent. The class teacher taunted Irvin, saying, "How can you love her now? You can't even see her face." Irvin and Pugalarasan felt disheartened at the moment, but they quickly decided to enjoy their last moments in the class. After thirty minutes, the name lists were delivered to the class teachers.

The students were divided into six classes: A, B, and C for boys, and D, E, and F for girls. The first floor was designated for girls, and the second floor for boys. Irvin and Phoebe didn't want this separation but had to adhere to the school rules. Now, the beautiful lovebirds were separated into different floors and classrooms.

Irvin couldn't concentrate on his studies due to the new atmosphere and rules of the school, particularly struggling with mathematics and continuously failing. Jeya

Krishnan was assigned to Section 'A', Pugalarasan and Irvin were assigned to Section 'B', and Nizam and other friends were assigned to Section 'C'.

Irvin felt he had lost both his crew and his love in the same year. However, Jeya Krishnan, Rashed Khan, Irvin, and Pugalarasan met during intervals. After school, Irvin and Rashed Khan waited at their usual spot to see Phoebe, while Pugalarasan, Nizam, and Jeya Krishnan went to see Logini.

After Phoebe went home with her mother, Irvin joined his friends behind the school with ice cream. Despite being separated by school regulations, they found ways to enjoy their lives. Everything went smoothly in their daily routines, but that wouldn't last forever.

One day, a senior Muslim student threatened Pugalarasan, demanding he leave Logini alone. The senior claimed, "From now on, she is my girlfriend, so don't follow her. If you dare, you will face the consequences." Pugalarasan was torn, unable to give up his love but also fearing a confrontation with the senior, which left him frustrated.

The next day, Pugalarasan told Irvin about the incident. Irvin couldn't tolerate the senior's attitude, so after a long discussion, they decided to go to their usual spot to see Logini. After school, Irvin and Pugalarasan went to the spot, but the senior and his friends were already there. The senior grabbed Pugalarasan's collar and began to threaten him seriously. Irvin, who had influence, was not touched. Irvin, bursting with anger, reported the incident to Mani Varma, who agreed to help.

The next day, Rajan left his XL bike at home, so after school, he took his bicycle and quickly went to pick up Mani Varma. Irvin, Mani, and Pugalarasan then went to the spot. Mani Varma spoke on Pugalarasan's behalf and demanded the senior leave both Logini and Pugalarasan alone. Initially, the senior refused, but when Mani went into a rage, he understood the seriousness of the situation.

As a result, Pugalarasan was free to see his girl. This incident spread to the other two classes: some respected Irvin, while others began to fear him. Irvin's popularity was restored due to this incident.

Chapter XIII

The Test of Perseverance

Irvin's Comeback?

In eighth grade, Irvin regained his popularity by assisting his friend Pugalarasan; however, his romantic life remained stagnant. At Tiny Flower School, boys are prohibited from entering the girls' floor, so Irvin and his friends would surreptitiously observe their girlfriends in the corridor during breaks. Eventually, the P.E.T. teachers discovered their behaviour.

One day, Irvin was caught red-handed. The P.E.T. teacher gestured for him to come over, but Irvin thought his friends were calling him and said, "Dude, can you please be quiet? I'm looking for her." When the P.E.T. teacher called him again, Irvin turned around and was stunned. The teacher didn't take it too seriously; he simply tapped Irvin on the back and warned him. Phoebe knew that Irvin was standing in the corridor to see her, but she refused to acknowledge him with her eyes.

After school, Irvin waited in the same spot to see Phoebe. However, she avoided looking at him, riding off on her scooter with her mother. She hesitated to meet his gaze out of shyness, leaving Irvin confused about whether she reciprocated his feelings.

This matter of love reached the teachers' ears. Some did not consider it serious, but others, especially Irvin's relative and Tamil teacher, took it seriously. Irvin struggled with math and Tamil, and whenever he scored poorly in Tamil, his teacher would scold him, saying, "You have no interest in studying, but you have time for love?" She would then hit him with a ruler. She conveyed this news to his brother, Shane, but to him, it was old news.

She also attempted to inform his mother, Maanya. Irvin was petrified because Maanya was vehemently opposed to romantic relationships. Irvin tried to signal his teacher not to tell his mother about this issue, while Maanya pressed the teacher to reveal what she was hiding about Irvin. Fortunately, the teacher changed the subject, allowing Irvin to breathe a sigh of relief.

Irvin is madly in love with Phoebe, admiring her beauty, intelligence, dancing skills, and more. She is primarily a classical dancer but is also adept at Western styles. According to Irvin, whether she dances classical or Western, he never closes his eyes when she performs at school sports events or annual day celebrations. Time passed swiftly, like a flash of lightning, and Irvin successfully completed eighth grade.

Irvin was promoted to ninth grade, but unfortunately, he learned that most of his friends had decided to transfer to another school. During that period, many students chose to change schools because, compared to Tiny Flower School, Selvama School had better infrastructure and provided rigorous training, enabling even slow learners to achieve decent grades.

Irvin tried to convince Rajan and Maanya to let him transfer as well, but they refused due to issues of availability and convenience. At first, Irvin worried about how he would manage the next academic year without Pugalarasan and his other friends. Slowly, however, he managed to overcome his fears.

As the new academic year began, the school management once again decided to shuffle the classes according to student performance. Irvin was moved from the 'B' section to the 'A' section. He was thrilled to find that many familiar faces were in his new class, especially Jeya Krishnan, who also remained in the 'A' section.

Irvin quickly adapted to the other boys and they enjoyed every minute of their school lives together. However, academically, Irvin began to decline due to the distraction of smartphones. At that time, smartphones were just being introduced in India. Rajan's assistant bought a Samsung Grand Prime from Singapore, which cost twenty thousand rupees—a significant amount back then. Irvin wanted to buy a Nokia Lumia, the first Windows smartphone, but Rajan refused. Rajan, unfamiliar with how to operate a smartphone, asked Irvin for help. Taking advantage of this, Irvin devised a plan to appropriate the smartphone for himself and successfully did so.

Irvin became addicted to his smartphone and lost focus on his studies. Most of his teachers were new and unaware of his potential, so they judged him superficially. Irvin's Tamil teacher was a very strict and ambitious woman who demanded discipline and high scores from her students. Due to Irvin's poor academic performance, she concluded that he was a slow learner and began scolding and beating him harshly. However, Irvin paid no attention to her reprimands, remaining deeply engrossed in his smartphone.

After every main examination—quarterly and half-yearly—the school management arranges parents and teachers meetings to monitor students' progress. Typically, parents visit the class teacher to receive the report card and discuss their child's performance. However, Irvin's Tamil teacher insisted that her students' parents visit her as well. Irvin disliked her attitude and decided to avoid meeting her. During the parents and teachers meeting, Irvin and Maanya visited his class teacher. They exited through the other side, successfully avoiding an encounter with the Tamil teacher.

The next day, the Tamil teacher was furious. She had a list of names, including Irvin's, of the ten students who had refused to meet her. As punishment, she ordered that these ten students stand outside the classroom for the entire day. While Irvin was used to standing outside, doing so for an entire day was particularly challenging.

They were only allowed back into the classroom during the lunch period. After school, Irvin rode his bicycle home but found it difficult to press the pedals. At first, he didn't mention the punishment to his parents, but the next day, he struggled to wake up for school and even to use the restroom because of the previous day's punishment. Finally, he confessed everything to his mother, Maanya.

Maanya reached her boiling point and vented her anger at her mother. In the afternoon, the class teacher called Maanya regarding Irvin's absence, but Maanya used the opportunity to express all her frustration. She said, "The Tamil teacher is behaving like a tyrant. If Irvin made a mistake, is it right to punish him like this? The boy is suffering, and this is how you treat students?" The class teacher then asked Maanya to meet with her to address the issue.

The following day, Maanya went to school in the afternoon, where she and the Tamil teacher engaged in a heated discussion. During the conversation, Maanya raised her voice and said, "That teacher is acting like a brute, treating us as if we're animals." These words angered the Tamil teacher. Suddenly, both the Tamil teacher and the class teacher asked Irvin and Maanya to stay. The Tamil teacher instructed Irvin to bring his Tamil test notebook.

The Tamil teacher became furious and escalated the issue to the principal. She complained about Irvin's disruptive behaviour and poor performance in his studies, noting that Irvin hadn't even been assigned a separate test notebook for Tamil. The principal, already irritated with Irvin, refused to consider Maanya's perspective. In the end, the principal issued a final warning: "If Irvin scores higher marks in the next examination, he can remain at this school. However, if he fails, the school management will issue a Transfer Certificate."

After this incident, Irvin and Maanya returned home. At their house, Maanya unleashed a torrent of words upon Irvin, leaving him unable to speak or stop her. She said, "Your brother Shane earns me pride and respect among the teachers, but you only bring me shame. I can't even defend you to them." These words deeply wounded Irvin. Angry with the school management, Irvin resolved to prove his capabilities. He channeled his frustration into his studies, particularly in Tamil, and Maanya supported him in achieving higher marks, reminiscent of the past. Every individual has a pivotal moment in their career, and this was Irvin's.

Irvin was given separate test notebooks for all subjects, and he scored impressive marks—ten out of nine and eight in all his tests. In the next major examination, Irvin achieved high scores across all subjects, demonstrating to his Tamil teacher who he truly was.

Chapter XIV

Irvin's Resolve

Year of Growth and Challenges.

During ninth grade, Irvin reduced his mischievous activities and began to concentrate on his studies. Whenever he thought about doing something mischievous, he remembered his mom's words and remained silent. During this time, all his subject teachers and class teachers acknowledged his efforts. The social studies teacher directly confessed to him, "I thought you were a disobedient student and a slow learner, but now you have impressed me by scoring good marks. Keep it up, Irvin." The Tamil teacher also started to understand Irvin and became friendly with him.

Due to his silence, the boys from sections 'B' and 'C' became best friends since they were mostly volleyball players. They easily gained fame in the school as well as recognition from teachers. However, Irvin wasn't concerned about this; his only goal was to achieve good marks in the tenth public examination and to prove his worthiness to Maanya.

But sometimes he engaged in mischievous activities with his best friends Rashed M, Jeya Krishnan, Nawaf, Thiyagarajan, and Hakim. Wherever they went, they went as a group, even to the restroom. In most of Shakespeare's plays, the clown characters play a vital role, and similarly, Irvin knew how to fight, taught by Kettapettai friends. Rashed M is a boxer, but the others didn't know how to fight and often escalated problems with their words. Irvin and Rashed M would then step in to resolve the situation.

Rashed M is a boxer and excellent at problem-solving. He is in charge of boxing competitions and the selection board. He wants Irvin to join the boxing competitions and practice with him. However, Rajan and Maanya disagree with joining any sports, especially since Maanya dislikes violent games. At Tiny Flower School, the P.E. teachers focus solely on winning volleyball competitions and are not concerned about other sports like boxing and handball. Consequently, the students on the volleyball team think they are heroes and begin to oppress and bully students from other sections.

But the heroes of class 'A' enjoyed their precious time in the classroom. During this period, Facebook began booming on social media because of memes and trolls involving cine actors, which fueled the rivalry between two actors' fan groups: Vijay and Ajith. Irvin is a die-hard Vijay fan, and Rashed M is a die-hard Ajith fan, so they gathered in groups to support their respective idols.

They often engaged in verbal wars, which sometimes escalated to using strong, offensive language in the classroom. Some might think this behavior is cringeworthy or question why they cared so much about actors, but in those days, being a fan of these stars was an intense emotion. Despite these distractions, Irvin and his friends successfully passed ninth grade and were promoted to tenth grade.

Chapter XV

The Defiant Stand

Irvin enjoyed his vacation with his friends at Kettapettai and then returned to school. The management decided not to shuffle the classes, so Irvin, Jeyakrishnan, Rashed M, Nawaf, and their friends were pleased with the news. Tiny Flower School primarily focuses on tenth and twelfth-grade students because they must sit for public examinations that determine their future paths. Shane scored high marks in the tenth grade, so Rajan and Maanya have the same expectations for Irvin. They emphasized to him the significance of this examination. Initially, Irvin kept a low profile and studied diligently to achieve better marks, but this behaviour didn't last long.

Irvin eagerly awaited the arrival of the newly appointed class teacher. When she entered the classroom, both of them were surprised because she had been his math teacher in seventh grade. However, she had a favourable opinion of Irvin, which made him happy.

In section 'A,' everyone likes Irvin because he is usually a hilarious guy. Sometimes, they respect him because of his temper. However, some people don't weigh his pros and cons; they simply enjoy hanging out with him, like Rashed M, Jeyakrishnan, Nawaf, Hakim, and Thiyagarajan. These friends create a small world of their own and live happily within it.

One day, students from classes 'B' and 'C' bullied Thiyagarajan during the break. At that time, Irvin and Rashed M were vibing out with other friends in the boys' restroom. Since the tenth-grade classrooms were on the second floor and the eleventh and twelfth-grade classrooms were on the ground floor, nobody questioned them except for the P.E.T teachers.

The bullies teased Thiyagarajan and slapped his right cheek. After the break, Thiyagarajan informed Irvin and Rashed M about the incident. Irvin wanted to help but remembered his mom's words and remained silent. Rashed M, always concerned about Thiyagarajan because he was a childhood friend and liked his innocent nature, felt protective.

Rashed M couldn't control his anger and confronted Arasu, the main bully in the group, while Irvin, Nawaf, and Hakim watched. Suddenly, the other bullies gathered around, confronting Rashed M. It looked like a pack of hyenas surrounding a lion with its cub. They threatened and warned Rashed M, saying, "Bro, you can't even touch us. Even if you gathered the whole 'A' section, we could easily demolish your friends. So don't you dare lift your head or raise your chest, understand?"

Rashed M felt helpless because about ten people had surrounded him. He restrained his anger by clenching his fists and moved away. Rashed M gave Irvin a strange look and remained silent for the next four hours. After school, Irvin went home and reflected on the incident. He analyzed the situation and deciphered Rashed M's strange look. Irvin understood it and felt ashamed of his inaction. Now, Irvin sought a way to take revenge. He wanted to avenge their actions without damaging his reputation, so he waited for the right moment to seek retribution for his friends.

Irvin confessed his reasons to Rashed M, and they began strategizing to defeat the bullies. However, each time they tried, they failed. Meanwhile, Irvin gained insight into the teachers' mentality toward students. He excelled in all subjects while continuing his mischievous acts. This time, instead of hating him, the teachers loved him, which became a significant advantage for Irvin.

One day, Irvin confessed his problem to Keshava at Kettapettai. Keshava was in Twelfth 'C,' a class notorious for its misbehavior because of him and his friends. Keshava, who loved to fight, eagerly offered to help Irvin and said, "Combining two classes to beat up one class? Irvin, tomorrow you grab someone from their class, and when they come, call us. We'll come and see what they dare to do against us." Irvin agreed to the plan.

The next day, Irvin and Rashed M searched for the right target, and one of the bullies mocked Irvin. Seizing the opportunity, Irvin punched him hard in the face. The bullies gathered around Irvin and Rashed M, while Thiyagarajan went to summon Keshava and his friends. At the right moment, Keshava and his friends arrived on the scene. The bullies were shocked to see the twelfth-grade big shots interfering in the fight. They had underestimated Irvin and were now surprised by his influence.

The bullies tried to defend themselves by accusing Irvin of hitting their friend, but Keshava replied, "You guys started the fight by hitting Irvin's friend." Keshava and his friends threatened them and issued a warning. Keshava said, "If this happens again, you guys will be dead meat!" The bullies, now afraid, agreed to their terms. The heroes of section 'A' celebrated their first victory and began planning to take over the dominant position despite their limited strength.

Chapter XVI

Crossroads of Fate

Irvin's Struggle

Irvin and his friends were now esteemed by their classmates and had gained popularity among juniors and teachers alike. On the other hand, Irvin's romantic life was quite complicated because he wasn't sure whether Phoebe reciprocated his feelings. They only saw each other after school ended. In the eighth grade, Irvin and Pugalarasan tried to communicate with their respective crushes through the help of their classmates and friends. Unfortunately, Pugalarasan spoke to the messenger on weekends without Irvin's knowledge.

The next day, the girl's parents complained about Pugalarasan's activities, but fortunately, Irvin avoided the issue. Irvin realized that the messenger concept was a failure, so he scratched his head and pondered alternative ways to communicate with Phoebe. Jeya Krishnan, Rashed M, Nawaf, Thiyagarajan, and Hakim noticed Irvin's predicament and decided to assist him.

During the P.E.T period, Irvin and his entire class played only two games: cricket and sponge dodgeball. For higher grade students, the administration scheduled two P.E.T periods per week. Irvin and his friends decided that one period would be dedicated to cricket and the other to dodgeball. On dodgeball day, Irvin, who owned the sponge ball, wrote his nickname, "The Boss," along with his section, on the ball.

On the playground, Jeya Krishnan threw a ball towards Phoebe's classroom. Confused by Jeya Krishnan's actions and apprehensive about disturbing the girls, Irvin hesitated. Despite this, Jeya Krishnan, along with the others, continued to throw balls at Phoebe's classroom. In the end, the P.E.T master noticed this behavior and approached to reprimand Jeya Krishnan and Irvin. However, Irvin and the others managed to manipulate him with their words and resolved the issue.

Meanwhile, Phoebe's class teacher learned of the incident and began an investigation with her students. She discovered the romantic relationship between Irvin and Phoebe. Since Phoebe was an exceptional student, the teacher mistakenly believed that it was Irvin who was infatuated with Phoebe, not the other way around.

Coincidentally, Phoebe's class teacher also taught English to Irvin's class. She was well aware that Irvin was the brother of the outstanding student Shane and was also familiar with Maanya.

The English teacher maintained her silence for a few days and observed Irvin and his friends to ascertain the veracity of the information. However, she eventually discovered that Irvin indeed harbored romantic feelings for Phoebe. Irvin's love story began in the sixth grade and continued to the present, but most teachers opposed his feelings and used a wooden or steel scale to punish him harshly.

However, by the tenth grade, Irvin gained a few supporters among the teachers, which made him quite happy. The English teacher consistently reprimanded him because of his crush on Phoebe. She would often narrate stories of failed romances to indirectly criticize Irvin. Despite Irvin scoring eighty percent in English, she never encouraged him and instead continued to scold him.

Irvin's class teacher encouraged him in his studies and always stood up for him. One day, Irvin could no longer tolerate his anger towards his English teacher. During lunch, when the class teacher was supposed to eat with the students in the classroom, Irvin, consumed by anger, said, "Ma'am, the English teacher is always scolding me and indirectly attacking me. I can't tolerate her actions. Why is she so concerned about my love life? If this behavior continues, I will not hesitate to break her car window."

The class teacher reported everything Irvin said, and his classmates supported him. As a result, the English teacher felt helpless and stopped scolding him and narrating love failure stories. From this segment, I have a question: why do these mortals associate their lives with others? Why do they compare their lives to those of other people? We created humans to worship us. We made different races according to their landscapes.

Personally, I am the one who decides their fate, not the lives of others. Even though Irvin's decisions shape his life journey, I am the one who creates the paths he follows. This applies not only to Irvin but to everyone. So remember this before you judge someone in your life.

Chapter XVII

Irvin's Just Deserts

During a short period, Irvin and Phoebe's love affair became known throughout the staff room. Most teachers ignored it except for the English and science teachers. The management's goal was to achieve a one hundred percent success rate, so the teachers were focused on that. Sometimes Irvin's teachers were kind to him, but other times they showed a harsh demeanor. Irvin particularly struggled with the social studies teacher. She had taught him in eighth grade. New to the school, she was young and attractive, yet rude and arrogant. If she disliked someone's attitude, she became furious, and the person would be in serious trouble. Irvin had numerous battle wounds on his body, such as on his ear and near his arms.

Irvin was a person determined to prove his capabilities to others. Typically, he showed little interest in studying social science. He had a rebellious streak against the social studies teacher, so he deliberately scored low marks to provoke her.

She noticed his plan and pinched him hard on the ears. After school, Shane and Irvin played together, which sometimes led to fights. When Shane tried to twist Irvin's ears, he noticed nail marks and realized what had happened.

The next day, Irvin and his social studies teacher were standing outside the principal's office due to Irvin's rude behavior. Suddenly, Shane appeared and began arguing with the teacher. He said, "Why are you punishing my brother so ruthlessly? Look at his right ear! It's badly wounded, and I can see your nail marks on it." She replied, "Why would I beat him unnecessarily? He deliberately provoked me!" Shane raised his voice again and said, "Your reasons may be valid, and you have the right to discipline him. He deserves it, but he doesn't deserve such ruthless treatment, Ma'am." She was amazed by his speech and followed.

I love testing Irvin's patience, so I placed another tragedy in his life path, and I am curious to see how he handles it this time. Nawaf, Rashed M, and Irvin always hang out around the school; they are never seen alone in the classroom or the corridor.

One day, Nawaf's belt broke because of his size. Nawaf asked Irvin and Rashed M to accompany him, and they agreed. The trio went to the office, paid the fee for the belt, and waited outside. The break was over, and it was time for the science period. According to Irvin's classmates, the science teacher is the prettiest in the school. While she is strict with students, she is less than the social studies teacher, so Irvin considers her harmless.

Irvin asks Nawaf, "Did you ask for permission for us?" Nawaf replies, "Yes." So, Irvin and Rashed M are carefree as they enter the classroom late. They chorus their excuse, but the teacher responds, "What time is it now? Where have you been all this time?" Irvin explains, "Ma'am, we went to buy a belt for Nawaf, and he said that you granted permission." Suddenly, the science teacher bursts out in anger and says, "I only granted permission for Nawaf."

Irvin and Rashed M are bewildered and exchange glances. The science teacher, now furious, grabs a special wooden stick and swiftly attacks Irvin and Rashed M. Irvin is confused by the whole situation and tries to explain, "Ma'am, we thought Nawaf asked for permission for us. We are extremely sorry for our actions." She hesitates to listen to Irvin's words and continues to beat Irvin and Rashed M simultaneously. Irvin reaches his boiling point; he clenches his fists, grits his teeth, and stands like a statue.

Irvin was furious with both the science teacher and Nawaf, and he kept clenching his teeth after she let him back into the classroom. The bell rang, the science teacher left, and the math teacher entered the class. Usually, Irvin made the classroom lively with his charm and enthusiasm. But this time, he was seething with anger, and she noticed it. She asked, "Irvin, are you okay, son? You look like a boiling volcano. Did something happen in the classroom?"

These words fueled Irvin's rage, and he erupted. Irvin confessed the incident to his math teacher with agony and anger, crying for twenty minutes. She calmed him down and allowed him to rest. Irvin's final words were, "I will not let this issue slide; I will get my justice, whatever it takes, and I will make her regret her actions."

At Tiny Flower School, the school day ends at 3:50 PM, but tenth and twelfth-grade students have to attend an additional hour of tuition. The management provides a twenty-minute break for this. Irvin and his friends went out of the school, and he sponsored twenty bucks for orange ice cream while lamenting about the incident. Suddenly, a student approached him and said, "The science teacher has summoned you to meet her now." Irvin had been waiting for this opportunity and ran to meet her.

Irvin went to the staff room, and the science teacher came out to meet him. She said, "The class teacher told me everything. I am very sorry, Irvin." Irvin's eyes blazed with anger as he responded, "Ma'am, this is what I tried to tell you in the classroom, but you never listened and were only interested in beating me."

She repeated, "I'm sorry, Irvin." But he ignored her apology and raised his voice, saying, "How could you punish someone without doing anything wrong? If I made a mistake, your punishment would be valid, but this is so unfair. How could you do this, Ma'am?" This time, she humbled herself and again asked for his forgiveness. Irvin said, "I was furious with you, but I forgive you this time. Don't do this again and be a good teacher."

Irvin walked proudly and recounted to his friends how she had begged for an apology. This time, not only his friends but also the entire boys' section recognized Irvin's resolve, and some of them were proud of him.

Chapter XVIII

The Price of Humiliation

Irvin and his friends became popular among their juniors, classmates, and teachers. Previously, Irvin gained notoriety in the worst possible way, but this time, the teachers concluded that while Irvin is mischievous, he also focuses on his studies. Even during the parent-teacher meeting, they gave positive feedback about Irvin to Maanya, who was pleased with his transformation.

While Irvin was in the tenth grade, Shane graduated from the school. Although Shane's name was well-remembered by the teachers, they were somewhat disappointed in him. Despite being brilliant in his studies, he ended up scoring lower marks due to personal illness. Shane struggled to overcome his drowsiness. Shane once shone like the sun, but now Irvin shines like the moon.

In Irvin's life, he frequently received punishment from his teachers for his mischievous behavior, but during this period, I orchestrated a little emotional rollercoaster with the help of his Kettapettai friends.

While Irvin was in the tenth grade, Keshava was in the twelfth grade, so both had to prepare for their public examinations. Keshava was a slow learner and had failed in most subjects. The management decided to hold a special class for slow learners during the study holidays. However, Keshava disliked this arrangement, so he took a leave, stayed at Irvin's home, and spent his time using mobile phones.

One day, Irvin went to school without his lunch. Since Shane was now in college, Maanya asked Keshava to bring lunch to Irvin. Lunch hour began at 12:20 p.m., and parents were allowed to leave lunch boxes with the watchmen, from whom students would collect their meals. Keshava took Irvin's bike (a Pulsar 135) and headed to Tiny Flower School. However, Keshava got caught up chatting with his friends and showing off Irvin's bike to his female classmates. Unfortunately, Keshava's class teacher spotted him, dragged him to the classroom, and confiscated Irvin's bike, smartphone, and pocket modem.

Irvin went down to pick up his lunch bag and noticed his bike parked nearby. He was shocked and confused about how it got there. Turning his head toward the staff room, he saw Keshava's class teacher scolding

Keshava. Curious about what was happening, Irvin approached Keshava and learned that his bike, smartphone, and pocket modem had been confiscated. Looking down, Irvin also noticed that Keshava was wearing his brand-new slippers. Completely bewildered, Irvin scratched his head, trying to figure out how to get his things back from Keshava's class teacher. However, Keshava promised Irvin that he would recover everything.

Meanwhile, Maanya grew increasingly worried about Keshava's disappearance, and his grandmother inquired about him. Maanya feared that he might have met with an accident, so she repeatedly called Irvin's smartphone, but no one answered, and eventually, the phone was switched off.

After some time, Shane returned home from college, and Maanya broke the shocking news to him that Keshava had been missing for five hours. Now, Shane and Keshava's friends were tensed, and Shane contacted Paraman and others to find Keshava at any cost. The Kettapettai friends immediately jumped on their motorbikes and began searching for Keshava.

Shane heads out to find Keshava and learns from Irvin's friends that both Irvin and Keshava are standing outside the staff room. Furious, Shane contacts his friends and asks them to come to the school. After school is over, Irvin and Keshava approach Keshava's class teacher. Irvin says, "Ma'am, this issue is between you and him, so I won't interfere. But these things belong to me, so please return them."

However, she refuses and says, "The principal is on leave today, so you can't get your belongings now. Come back in two days." Irvin is furious with both Keshava and the class teacher and decides that he will leave the school with his things, no matter what.

The Kettapettai friends arrived at the school and argued with the watchman to let them inside. The watchman, feeling tensed, went to the staff room and informed the staff that some boys were causing trouble. One of the staff members spoke to the Kettapettai friends and said, "Don't create any problems here. If you cause chaos, your friends will face the consequences. So, kindly leave the premises."

Irvin met his Kettapettai friends and, seeing the situation, asked them to wait outside without causing a scene. They complied and waited. A few minutes later, Shane arrived at the school, tensed and fuming like a pressure cooker, and headed straight for the staff room. For the first time, Irvin and Keshava were genuinely afraid of him. Shane approached Irvin to get the full story and then shot a furious glance at Keshava.

As mentioned, Shane was well-known among the teachers, and everyone knew his name. Keshava's class teacher, who was also a former teacher of Shane, met him and mocked him in front of everyone for his weaknesses. This encounter was another opportunity for Shane to exact his revenge. Shane seized the chance and began to argue with her. He raised his voice and said, "Ma'am, whatever actions you took might be justified, but you should have informed his parents, right? We've been searching for him for an hour and were worried sick, and yet you turned off the damn smartphone. How can you be so irresponsible?"

Irvin and Keshava were genuinely amazed. Keshava's class teacher was deeply unsettled by Shane's words and felt that Shane was humiliating her in front of others. Overwhelmed, she ran into the staff room crying. After a few minutes, Shane felt remorseful and went to apologize, but she shouted, "Who asked you to come here? GET OUT!" Shortly after, a new teacher took over the situation. She calmed Shane, returned Irvin's bike, and persuaded him to leave. She assured him that their belongings would be returned in two days.

Irvin was upset about his smartphone and pocket modem being left on the principal's desk. However, he was thrilled by Shane's impressive performance at the school. This behavior was astonishing to the Kettapettai friends, as Shane was usually a calm boy who never involved himself in others' problems. But this time, Shane stood up for his brother and his friend Keshava.

I observed that Shane was humiliated by Keshava's class teacher in front of others, and he confided in Maanya about it multiple times. Now, I have devised a revenge plot to make her regret her actions. "You reap what you sow. Once you have tasted salt, you must drink water."

Chapter XIX

Harmony Amidst Conflict

The Irvin Chronicles

For two days, Irvin felt troubled because his smartphone and pocket modem were stuck at school due to Keshava's actions. However, he also felt proud to have seen a different side of Shane. Teachers had always praised Shane for his kindness and disciplined behavior, while they treated Irvin like a villain. Irvin had always thought of Shane as a coward and a nerd, but now his perception had completely changed. After two days, Irvin and Keshava waited outside the principal's office. The principal privately warned Keshava and returned the confiscated items to him. This brought great relief to both Irvin and Keshava as they headed home.

Irvin and his friends were starting to dominate the boys' floor. However, on the other side, their rivals were eager to get revenge and reclaim their status. They remained quiet for a while, but as Irvin and his friends' reputation grew, jealousy began to brew among the other boys. They devised a plan to bring down Irvin and his group.

One day, the rivals deliberately provoked Rashed M in the middle of the corridor, leading to a heated argument. Irvin was with Nawaf, watching Phoebe, when Rashed M approached them and reported everything that had happened. Irvin and Rashed M decided to take on the entire crew without seeking help from their seniors or their Kettapettai friends. They knew the odds of winning were slim, but they were determined to give it their all.

After school, they met outside near the bicycle racks, where the confrontation quickly escalated. The groups began arguing in Tamil, hurling insults at each other. Irvin, Rashed M, Nawaf, and Hakim prepared to fight against the ten members of the opposing group.

Unexpectedly, Mani Varma arrived on the scene and noticed that Irvin and his friends were surrounded by a group of boys. Mani Varma intervened and asked Irvin, "What's going on?" Irvin, asked surprisigly, "What are you doing here?" Mani Varma replied, "I saw a beautiful girl and followed her, and I ended up here. Then I saw you, dummy." Irvin quickly explained the situation to him.

Mani Varma, furious at the group of boys, began threatening them, saying, "If you touch Irvin or his friends again, I swear we'll come back and break your faces, no matter what." After this, everyone dispersed, but the nearby shopkeepers noticed the incident and reported it to the teachers.

The next day, Irvin and his friends entered the classroom with pride, only to be met with a scolding from their science teacher. "Are you goons or students? Who gave you the right to fight your classmates and involve outsiders in your conflicts?" This time, however, Irvin and his friends paid no attention to her lecture, feeling proud of the incident instead.

After a few weeks, Irvin and his friends realized that their time in tenth grade was coming to an end, so they decided to make peace with their rivals and unite to rule the boys' floor together. During the evening break, Irvin and his friends met with the leader of the opposing group, and after a ten-minute conversation, they agreed to a compromise, merging into one group with shared authority. This arrangement pleased the opposing team, and they became friends. A week into their newfound friendship, they embarked on their first mission together: to sabotage the security cameras.

At Tiny Flower School, the management believed that some students were getting out of hand, so they decided to issue Transfer Certificates (TC) to those students with proper evidence. To monitor the students closely, they installed cameras in all the classrooms. The principal watched them daily, as keenly as an eagle watches its prey. Irvin often sported a rugged look—his shirt untucked, the first button undone, and his tie worn to his fit but in a careless manner.

One day, during the Morning Prayer, everyone recited the prayer in unison. Irvin, being a Puritan, refused to participate in the Roman Catholic prayer and remained silent with his eyes open, standing quietly in the corner of the bench. From the principal's office, she noticed Irvin not participating and called him out through the microphone, humiliating him in front of the entire school. This public embarrassment deeply affected Irvin, and his friends took the matter seriously.

After school ended, as students hurried to leave for home, Irvin's friends from the 'B' section discreetly covered their faces with handkerchiefs and turned the camera towards the wall, ensuring the principal couldn't monitor them again. The next day, the head of the teachers called students from sections A, B, and C to assemble for an inquiry into the incident. Some students were shocked and had no idea who was responsible, but they suspected that Irvin's friends were involved.

The teachers threatened the students, saying, "Reveal the culprit, and I'll let you have lunch; otherwise, you won't be allowed to eat." Irvin feared that someone might step forward and disclose the responsible parties, but fortunately, no one did. Instead, everyone remained silent. The teachers made several attempts to find out who was behind it but ultimately failed and decided to drop the matter. Irvin and his new friends took pride in their unity and the successful handling of the situation.

Now, Irvin has no enemies and no more restroom fights. Instead, they drum in the restroom, creating their own beats and lyrics while dancing. Irvin and his friends thoroughly enjoy this phase and become role models for incoming students.

Chapter XX

From Shadows to Stardom

Irvin's School Saga

As the tenth-grade boys approached the climax of their school life, Irvin, Jeya Krishnan, and Rashed Khan dedicated themselves to studying hard in preparation for their exams. They planned a group study session at Irvin's home that night. Since most of Irvin's friends were slow learners and he had some lingering doubts, he decided to bring his friends to school on his motorbike for extra study time.

They reviewed additional subject material and took breaks to play at school. When the public examinations began, the school management arranged two government buses—one for boys and one for girls—to transport students to the exam center. Before the exams, they knelt in prayer, asking God for guidance and success.

After the final examination, the teachers held a meeting and reviewed a list of top students. And guess what? Irvin's name topped the list! Following the exams, the students were filled with enthusiasm, celebrating by bursting crackers outside the school—or sometimes even tossing them into the school grounds.

Keshava's class was responsible for these disturbances, so the principal decided to compile a list of troublesome students and instructed their parents to pick them up to prevent further incidents. Nawaf and several other parents arrived at the exam center and picked up their children. However, Irvin and Rashed M were left at the school because Maanya was ill, and Rashed M's parents were occupied with work.

True friends never leave you behind in any situation. Nawaf went to Irvin's home to deliver the message and was asked to pick up Irvin. Nawaf traveled about seven kilometers and explained to his social teacher, "Ma'am, Irvin's mother is ill and cannot pick him up, so she asked me to do it." The teacher was skeptical and refused to let Irvin go with him. After some time, they decided to send Irvin and Rashed M on the girls' bus to get them to school.

Irvin and Rashed M were thrilled because Irvin could see Phoebe, and Rashed could see other beautiful girls. However, the teacher kept a close watch on them, so they couldn't freely enjoy the sight of the girls.

After they reached the school, everyone went back to their homes. Irvin was troubled because he had two things on his mind: first, he and his friends wanted to burst crackers outside the school, and second, he wanted to confess his love to Phoebe again. Unfortunately, both plans were thwarted by the list of names.

Irvin and Rashed M were left alone on the school campus, and the teachers contacted their respective parents to pick them up. After some time, Rashed M's father, Iqbal, arrived and took him home. A few minutes later, Irvin's sick mother, Maanya, arrived by auto and picked him up. Irvin realized that the school year had come to an end. He knew he wouldn't see his group again and began to feel nostalgic during the vacation period.

One month later, the state government announced the date for the public examination results for tenth and twelfth grade students. When the day arrived, Irvin and his parents prayed to God for high marks and hoped he would be selected for a top spot in the school.

Usually, during this period, parents are more anxious than the students about their children's futures.

Other relatives pressure the parents to find out the marks and compare them with their own children's results. This frustrating behavior has persisted for generations. However, prayers are not in vain. Irvin achieved high marks, and surprisingly, Rashed Khan scored the same. Jeya Krishnan outperformed both Irvin and Rashed Khan.

After the results, Irvin's parents were deciding whether to transfer him to another school or keep him in the same one. They are also considering different subject groups for him. Meanwhile, Irvin and Jeya Krishnan are planning to join a Polytechnic College and find a job as soon as possible. Rajan disapproves of Irvin's plan and restricts him to only two subject options: biology or computer science.

Irvin's life went more smoothly during the vacation period. He often hung out with his Kettapettai friends, who would visit his house late at night. During this time, Irvin encountered two incidents. One day, while traveling to New Fort with Maanya for a prayer meeting, he received a message from an anonymous number.

Irvin didn't know who it was, so he asked, "Who are you?" However, the other person refused to reveal their identity and kept sending him messages. This continued for two weeks, and Irvin still had no idea who it was. He suspected his Kettapettai friends, so he asked them to reveal themselves, but they were confused and didn't understand what he was talking about.

One day, Irvin shared his frustration with his neighbor, a sister, who suggested, "Download the Truecaller app from the Play Store, enter the anonymous number, and you'll find out who it is." Irvin quickly took out his phone, downloaded the app, and entered the number into the search box.

His neighbor, Shane, and Irvin eagerly awaited the result. Irvin was stunned when he saw the name—it was Phoebe, who had been tormenting him for two weeks. Overwhelmed with joy, Irvin began acting ecstatic— shouting, jumping, and unable to keep his feet on the ground.

Irvin's long-time dream comes true. Soon after, Phoebe starts playing hide-and-seek with him. Irvin replies with "Hello, baby," accompanied by a love emoji. At first, Phoebe is surprised by how he managed to find her, but they gradually developed their relationship through their smartphones.

Chapter XXI

The Final Chapter of Tiny Flower School

From Schoolyard Struggles to New Horizons

During the vacation, Irvin and Phoebe deepened their romantic relationship through WhatsApp messages. However, they avoided going on dates or engaging in typical activities for their age group. The most Irvin would do was to pass by Phoebe's house on his motorbike, where she would stand on the veranda. He would catch a glimpse of her face for just four seconds, but to him, it felt like watching a slow-motion video. Each time he saw her, his happiness soared. Irvin was elated that Phoebe had fallen for him.

Like many couples, they shared the details of their day with each other. Everything seemed perfect, except for Irvin's strong desire to see Phoebe on a video call. Unfortunately, Phoebe declined due to her coyness. Everything was going smoothly during the vacation. Rajan and Maanya decided to continue Irvin's studies at Tiny Flower School and chose computer science for him, as Irvin was not strong in drawing.

In Kettapettai, some of Irvin's friends used to drink alcohol, but Irvin didn't have this habit. However, he would join them for fun and enjoy the side dishes. If his friends brought alcohol, they would also bring non-vegetarian items like chicken curry, beef curry, and botti. The truth is, drinking alcohol and eating non-vegetarian dishes together gives an extra kick. Irvin loved non-vegetarian food, so he would end up eating most of the dishes, leaving insufficient portions for the others. They would get angry and scold Irvin with harsh words, but he would just ignore them and savor the moment.

Irvin didn't like consuming alcohol under any circumstances, so he never appreciated its presence. He also avoided interfering in others' choices, even when it came to his closest friends. One day, while one group of Irvin's friends went to buy alcohol, another group collected money from everyone to purchase side dishes. This time, they had decided in advance not to buy non-vegetarian items because of Irvin. A total of twenty people gathered at a local shop, where they asked the shopkeeper to buy snacks to use as side dishes.

Suddenly, two police officers arrived in Kettapettai and noticed a crowd near the petty shop. As they approached, some people spotted them and quickly dispersed, prompting the officers to leave without conducting any inquiries. However, the officers found Irvin's bike suspicious, as it appeared to be stolen, so they stopped him on the road and began questioning him. They asked him to provide the RC book. Irvin had a soft copy of the RC folded and stored in his bike bag, but unfortunately, it had been torn into pieces due to the rain. He handed the two torn pieces of paper to the police officer.

Irvin didn't intend to mock the officers. However, he was worried because he had two bottles of alcohol inside his bike's bag and feared they might be confiscated. The police officer, now furious, demanded, "Where do you live?" Irvin responded, "It's nearby, sir." The officers instructed him to go home and bring back either the original or a clear soft copy of the RC book to prove ownership of the bike. They temporarily seized his bike and kept it at the primary government hospital.

Irvin hurried home to retrieve the RC book. Meanwhile, his friends attempted to retrieve the alcohol bottles from his bike, but the officers had already confiscated them, along with Keshava's smartphone. When Irvin reached home, he called out to his mom, but unfortunately, she was at a prayer meeting at the church, leaving only Shane at home.

Irvin confessed everything to Shane, and together they searched for the RC book. After some time, they found it and headed back to the spot, but the police were not there, so they waited for over forty-five minutes. Irvin's friends stood at a distance, trying to contact influential people to help recover the bike, the alcohol, and Irvin. It was a bad day for Irvin. When the police officers returned, they asked, "Who is he?" Irvin replied, "He's my brother."

They began scolding Irvin, and Shane tried to defend him. They chorused for him to shut up, saying, "You look like a junkie." Irvin laughed to himself because Shane never even sat with his friends when they consumed alcohol.

During this conversation, a church member arrived on the scene and asked the officers to release Irvin and Shane, vouching for their good character. However, the police officers responded, "Sir, he has alcohol in his bike." The church member was at a loss for words and felt disappointed in both Irvin and Shane.

Irvin and Shane were worried that if news of this incident spread to the church, it would tarnish their reputations and reflect poorly on Maanya's upbringing. The police officers decided to take Irvin into custody along with his bike. However, they treated him fairly at the station, offering him a chair to sit on rather than making him squat, which is usually the norm for those in custody. They began by inquiring about his age and school. Irvin responded, "I completed tenth grade at Tiny Flower School." When they asked his name, he answered, "Irvin."

One of the police officers revealed that the principal had provided them with a list of students' names, with Irvin's name at the top. Irvin, taken aback, quickly fabricated a story, claiming that the bottles did not belong to him but to his cricket mate.

Irvin struggled to convince them with his story. Although they believed him, they refused to release him. As night fell, Maanya returned home from the prayer meeting. Shane then informed her about the afternoon's events. Furious, Maanya went to the police station alone. Knowing she was coming, Irvin asked the officers not to mention the alcohol bottles to his mother. They agreed.

Maanya arrived at the police station and began to berate the officers. Unable to withstand her anger, they revealed the truth: "Indha ma un pulla vandi la sarakku vechurukan." (Your son has stored liquor on his bike) Maanya was shocked and shouted at Irvin, who attempted to explain himself. In the end, she offered a bribe of five hundred rupees to the officers. However, they refused, saying, "Indha neegalae vechukoga, unga paiyana kaali pasangaloda sera vidathiga." (Kept it yourself, don't let your son hang out with goons).

Irvin retrieved his seized items, except for the alcohol bottles. He and his mother returned home with his bike. Once they arrived, Maanya scolded Irvin, and he retold the same story he had used with the police. Maanya was persuaded and offered him advice.

Later, Irvin revealed that the principal had provided the list of troublesome students to the police. This information only fuelled Maanya's anger further. She became more enraged and confided in her husband, Rajan, who always supported Irvin. Maanya exclaimed, "How could she be so cruel? Who gave her the authority to turn over names to the police?" She wanted to confront the principal at school, but she knew that if they asked for anything from the school, it would likely be denied. So, they decided to remain silent and plan to change schools.

Irvin loved his school dearly, but now he had a reason to leave. So, the whole family began searching for a new school for Irvin's higher studies. Thus, the saga of Tiny Flower School comes to an end……

Chapter XXII

Navigating Change

Irvin and the Ties that Bind

Maanya was enraged by the actions of the Tiny Flower School principal. Although several schools reached out to Maanya, offering to admit her son, Irvin, she declined due to their exorbitant fees and unsuitable teaching methods. Maanya's anger was also directed at Irvin, whose disobedience had led the principal to report him to the police, bringing disgrace upon the family. Despite Maanya's insistence, Rajan listened patiently but refused to punish Irvin.

From the outset of Irvin's life, Rajan never resorted to physical punishment for his sons; he limited his discipline to verbal reprimands. Rajan harbored a special affection for Irvin, even more so than for Shane. In Tamil films, the protagonist often lacks a close relationship with his father, creating a stereotype among Tamil people. However, in this story, Irvin and Rajan shared a deep bond that resembled a friendship more than a typical father-son relationship. They conversed casually, with phrases like "Dai appa, enna da pannura," (More causal talk) yet Irvin refrained from such informal speech in public, particularly in the presence of relatives.

From childhood, Shane never asked his father to buy anything and maintained clear boundaries with Rajan. He shared a closer relationship with Maanya. In contrast, Irvin was the complete opposite. When Irvin requested something, Rajan would initially refuse, but Irvin would eventually have it in his hands. However, Rajan was now concerned about Irvin's future and entrusted him with the responsibility of finding a suitable school for his admission. During his search, Irvin encountered his childhood friend Robin and sought his advice on the best schools in Thendralpalli.

Robin, with a flash of insight, recommended his own school, which was located quite far from Irvin's home. Irvin, feeling uncertain, sought Maanya's counsel. She advised him to take his time before making a decision. Meanwhile, Irvin was anxious, having attended Tiny Flower School from lower kindergarten through tenth grade, where he was deeply familiar with his classmates and teachers. At Robin's school, he only knew one person—Robin himself—and felt uneasy about forming friendships with strangers. Irvin found himself in a dilemma: should he remain at the school that had reported him to the police and branded him as a culprit, or should he enroll in a new, unfamiliar environment?

Two days later, Maanya decided to enroll Irvin in Robin's school. She advised him to be kind and obedient, warning him not to bring any embarrassment to her. These words stung Irvin, and he resolved to remain calm and gentle, mentally preparing himself to spend the next two years as a nerd student.

A few days afterward, Irvin, Maanya, and Robin visited the school. After a short wait, Irvin and Maanya were ushered into the headmistress's office. The headmistress scrutinized Irvin's appearance and reviewed the marks he had scored in his public examinations. After delivering a lengthy speech, she granted him admission to Robin's school, where he would major in computer science. Irvin was thrilled because this school was significantly larger than Tiny Flower School. It even hosted a carnival on its grounds, and Irvin was eagerly looking forward to his first day.

The day finally arrived, and Irvin came early to his new school with Robin. However, after the school assembly ended, Irvin felt deceived. The school's low student population contrasted sharply with the exorbitant fees they had to pay, comparable to Tiny Flower's fees. In this new school, the computer science group was considered the premier group, but once again, Irvin felt betrayed. Despite the school being co-educational, his class was comprised entirely of boys, and the class size was small. This made Irvin furious, and he quickly began to dislike the school. From that point on, Irvin gradually forgot how to interact with girls and developed anxiety when approaching them.

After starting at his new school, Irvin lamented to Maanya, pleading with her to help him transfer, but she refused. Over the next two years, Irvin faced many unpleasant experiences. The older students began to tease and belittle him, unaware of his past, but Irvin clenched his fists and maintained a nerdy facade. He genuinely missed his old school and close friends. During math class, he imagined how the students at Tiny Flower School would laugh if they saw his nerdy act. However, amidst these challenges, he found some valuable friends in Vimal, Kaasi, Waafir, and Judas.

Vimal, Kaasi, Waafir, and Judas were also new to the school and shared similar feelings with Irvin, who quickly bonded them as best friends. Irvin, Vimal, Kaasi, and Waafir would hang out during breaks and eat lunch together under the shelter of a tree. However, Judas often declined to join them, partly due to his reluctance to walk long distances and partly because of his fear of being reprimanded by teachers. Despite his imposing appearance, Judas had a playful, almost comical personality.

These five became inseparable, enjoying life together by going to the theater, exploring restaurants for exotic dishes, borrowing Rashed Khan's camera to take pictures for Instagram, and, most importantly, spending time at Vimal's house. Since Vimal's parents were often away, they would order Domino's pizza and non-alcohol fruit beer or sometimes buy chicken by the kilogram and cook it themselves.

Chapter XXIII

New Year's Despair

Irvin's Love Lost Amidst Celebration Chaos

Irvin spent two years at his new school, living as though he were a nerd. Meanwhile, Phoebe excelled in her tenth-grade public examinations, securing third place overall in the school. However, in pursuit of a superior education, Phoebe's parents decided to enroll her at SVS School. Prior to Irvin's admission to his new school, Phoebe urged him to join SVS School so they could remain in each other's company. Given that their bus route would be the same, she assured him that they would never be alone.

SVS School, however, was known for its stringent policies, particularly towards students like Irvin, making it a challenging environment to endure for two years. The school was infamous for not declaring holidays on Saturdays and even on certain government-mandated holidays, focusing exclusively on academics with little regard for extracurricular activities. Phoebe's plead moved Irvin, yet he ultimately declined to join SVS School.

Irvin and Phoebe attended different schools, but they now had smartphones to stay in touch. Irvin's school day ended at 4:30 PM, while Phoebe's concluded at 5 PM. However, she usually waited at her bus stop from 5:30 to 5:45 PM. As for Judas, he would vanish with his father immediately after the final bell rang.

Irvin, Kaasi, Waafir, and Vimal hurried out of the school and walked approximately one kilometer to reach the central bus station. Irvin had to wait thirty minutes for his bus to Kettapettai. To avoid the delay, he decided to take two different buses to reach Kettapettai as quickly as possible to see Phoebe. Upon arriving home, Irvin swiftly dropped his bag, removed his shoes, dashed into the bathroom to wash his face, and then grabbed his bike key before heading to the bus station to meet Phoebe. Irvin's love life had been going smoothly, despite his new school feeling like a living nightmare.

He was completely infatuated with Phoebe. One day, Maanya discovered a passport-sized photo and showed it to Irvin, asking, "Who is she, and how did this photo end up in your locker?" Irvin was petrified and unsure how to navigate the situation. She gave him a stern warning. A year earlier, Niwaf had drawn a large heart in his notebook and written "Irvin loves Phoebe" inside it.

When Irvin saw the drawing, he immediately tore up the paper and left it in his room. Maanya and Rajan had a habit of checking papers before discarding them in the dustbin. As usual, Maanya opened the torn paper and saw the writing. She was furious and scolded Irvin harshly. Irvin was at a loss and didn't know how to handle the situation. He turned to his friends for advice, and they told him, "Distance yourself from Phoebe for a while, or your mother will make your life miserable."

Now, Maanya closely monitored Irvin's activities, leaving him unable to think clearly due to the pressure. Irvin confided in Phoebe, and they mutually decided to end their relationship. Although Irvin disliked his decision and felt a heavy weight in his heart, he deliberately portrayed himself as a bad person to Phoebe. Phoebe cried a great deal and tried to convince Irvin to reconsider, but she couldn't grasp the turmoil he was experiencing. Thus, Irvin's once-beautiful love story came to an end.

As a result, Irvin began to behave arrogantly. If someone stared at him, he would turn his motorbike around, confront the person, and beat them before quickly fleeing the scene. Occasionally, this led to bigger conflicts, but the influential figures in Kettapettai would resolve the issues without his parents finding out. The once-jovial Irvin had transformed into a serious, arrogant, and withdrawn individual.

Irvin's friends in Kettapettai noticed his miserable state and decided not to leave him alone. Wherever they went, Irvin was always with them. After a few months, Irvin began to heal from his emotional breakdown, thanks to the support of his friends. Without them, it might have taken years for him to recover, potentially causing long-term effects on his mental health.

Fortunately, despite his difficult journey, Irvin never turned to alcohol as a coping mechanism. Now, Irvin and Phoebe have gone their separate ways, walking their own life paths and never crossing each other's. For every Christian, Christmas and New Year are significant festivals, and they never fail to attend church services.

However, in 2019, Irvin's friends from Kettapettai persuaded Shane and Irvin to skip the New Year service and spend time with them instead. Initially, Shane was hesitant, fearing the consequences if Maanya discovered their actions. Despite his reservations, the Kettapettai friends convinced him to accept their invitation. Without Maanya's or Rajan's knowledge, Shane and Irvin skipped the service and began hanging out with their friends.

On December 31st, the friends from Kettapettai gathered at Irvin's den. Nearly thirty members assembled with their motorbikes. As they rode out from Kettapettai, the sound of the roaring motorcycles amazed and intimidated everyone in the streets. They brought a large cake for two reasons: to celebrate the New Year and to mark Jeya Krishnan's birthday, which fell on the same day. It was meant to be the best New Year celebration and a special birthday party for Jeya Krishnan.

In that group, most of Irvin's friends were drunk and intoxicated. During the New Year celebrations, many of them died due to their condition. Consequently, the government instructed the police to patrol the streets and disperse those celebrating on the roadsides. The group stopped near Kaveri Bank, where Mani Varma had brought some homemade fireworks. He set them off on the road while shouting "Happy New Year" and waving to passing motorists.

Suddenly, they heard a siren and saw a police car approaching. Thrilled and anxious, they quickly mounted their motorbikes to escape. At that moment, Aamir's foot slipped, and he was on the verge of falling into a slope that led to the river. Aamir grabbed Irvin's T-shirt, but Irvin, panicked by the approaching siren, failed to notice Aamir's grip. He shouted, "Dai yaara sattaiya pudichu ezhukurathu mairan, vanthu vandi la eru da." (Hey, who are you pulling by the shirt, idiot? Come and get on the vehicle.) Irvin rushed to retrieve his bike, causing Aamir to lose his grip and tumble down the slope. Paraman saw this and quickly rescued Aamir. They managed to leave the scene in just fifteen minutes.

Everyone who witnessed the incident burst into laughter. They then traveled to the longest bridge in Thendralpalli, shouting, "Happy New Year!" Simultaneously, Paraman's friends arrived at the scene with their van. They played popular folk songs and danced to the music. In total, about fifty people had gathered there. Meanwhile, due to his over-enthusiasm, Mani Varma threw a homemade firework into the air, but unfortunately, it fell among the crowd.

Everyone fled from the firework and cursed Mani Varma for his actions. However, he took their reactions as encouragement and threw another firework into the air.

This time, it landed on the roof of a private bus and exploded. The crowd erupted with joy, and it turned out to be the most memorable and final New Year celebration in their history.

After the New Year celebration, they arrived at Irvin's home at 3:00 AM, and some of his friends decided to stay the night. Consequently, fifteen people filled all the available spaces in Irvin's house.

Chapter XXIV

The Unexpected Ties that Bind

Unexpected twists and turns defined Irvin's life. As I've mentioned before, life is linked to a blood pressure monitor; the line will rise and fall, never remaining perfectly stable. No mortal can maintain a constant equilibrium in their life. That's where my system comes into play. I offer numerous paths for your journey, but it is you, humans, who choose which one to follow to navigate the rest of your lives. In this instance, Irvin opted to forge his own path without Phoebe by his side.

Irvin successfully completed his higher grades and was now prepared to enter college. In the final months of their twelfth grade, Irvin, Vimal, Judas, and Waafir deliberated on which courses to pursue in college. The four of them struggled with mathematics, leading them to decide on majoring in English. Vimal and Judas consistently lauded one institution above all others: Benjamin Herbert College.

One of the most prestigious colleges in Thendralpalli, Benjamin Herbert College was largely unknown to Irvin, but Judas and Vimal built up its reputation for him. Now, Irvin, Judas, and Vimal were eager to enroll. Meanwhile, Waafir also chose to major in English but preferred to attend a different college.

At Benjamin Herbert College, admission is reserved for students with exceptional marks. Irvin, Judas, and Vimal were well aware that achieving such scores at their current school was unlikely. Before the school year concluded, Judas reached out to influential figures in the church and secured two letters of recommendation. Vimal's parents had strong connections with the college principal, ensuring his acceptance into the college.

Irvin was unaware of these arrangements. However, he was close to Vimal's family, and since Vimal's mother was also a teacher at the same school, they often turned to her whenever they needed assistance. Irvin had great faith in Vimal's parents and asked them for a recommendation.

Despite their efforts, the applications for Irvin, Judas, and Vimal were initially rejected. However, they directly approached the principal and secured a seat for Vimal. Judas also managed to obtain a seat through his recommendation letter. Now, Vimal's parents called Irvin, asking him to come to the college with Maanya.

Irvin and Maanya arrived at the college, where Vimal's parents warmly greeted Maanya. Irvin held only an application form in his hand, with no recommendation letter. He was terrified of not gaining admission to the college, especially since he had boasted about it to his Kettapettai friends. If he failed, the entire group would mock him.

Irvin had been discussing his admission with Vimal's mother for the past two months, so they were determined to help him secure a spot. Vimal's father, an alumnus of the college, reached out to some of his friends who were now professors there. However, when he asked one of them for assistance, they declined to offer Irvin a seat in English and instead suggested he join the Physics program at the same college.

Irvin and Maanya believed, "Physics must be God's will." However, Irvin was directed to Gayathri Ma'am for admission. Now, he was more terrified than ever, unsure if he would be accepted into the college or return to Kettapettai with a heavy heart. Irvin and Vimal's father went to the admissions office. Vimal's father introduced them and asked Irvin to hand the admission slip to her. Gayathri Ma'am reviewed his marks and granted him admission for a BA in English. Irvin was overjoyed to have secured a place at the prestigious college and looked forward to spending the next three years with his friends, Judas and Vimal.

Everyone was delighted that Irvin had gained admission and would be studying alongside their children. Vimal's parents and Judas's mother were discussing their hometowns when Maanya overheard and began to inquire further. In the course of the conversation, they discovered that Irvin and Vimal were not just friends but also relatives. This revelation was a complete surprise to Irvin and Vimal, leaving them unsure how to respond, so they started acting awkwardly. Vimal's parents were thrilled to uncover this new family connection.

Chapter XXV

The Chronicles of a Day Filled with Surprises and Unplanned Escapades

Irvin, Judas, and Vimal successfully enrolled at Benjamin Herbert College. On their first day, Irvin was unfamiliar with the surroundings, but Vimal, who was well-known on campus, invited Irvin to explore the college. They asked Judas to hold their seats in the classroom. While they were away, a student entered the room and noticed the spot where Irvin had reserved his seat. Judas informed him that the seat was already taken, but the student, skeptical, sat down in Irvin's spot anyway. When Irvin and Vimal returned to the classroom, Irvin noticed someone else's bag in his seat and was confused. Without hesitation, Irvin picked up the bag and tossed it aside.

A peculiar-looking guy entered the classroom, searching for his bag. Irvin initially thought he seemed rugged and arrogant, expecting him to confront him about the bag. However, the guy, who looked more like a nerd, simply retrieved his bag without saying a word and quietly went to his seat. A few minutes later, the class teacher arrived, introduced herself, and asked the students to introduce themselves—a task Irvin found particularly annoying.

During the self-introduction session, each student shared their name and where they were from. The nerdy guy introduced himself as Venkat, mentioning that he was a local from Thendralpalli. When it was Irvin, Judas, and Vimal's turn to introduce themselves, everyone turned to look at them. This was because the class was filled with students from diverse backgrounds, but these three had not only attended the same school but had also enrolled in the same college, chosen the same major, and were on the same shift. As a result, the teachers easily remembered their names.

After a few days, Irvin, Judas, and Vimal began to grow bored of college, finding nothing there that captured their interest, and they struggled to socialize with others. As a result, the three of them started skipping classes, riding their bikes around outside of the college campus, and occasionally heading home instead. This routine continued for months, with them even taking days off together and spending their time at home.

The class teacher noticed Irvin, Judas, and Vimal's irregular attendance and observed their activities. One day, she called Irvin and Judas to the staff room. Irvin was confused about why she had summoned them, while Judas was terrified. When they arrived at the staff room and met her, she glared at them furiously and began questioning them about their absences during class periods and their habit of taking leave on the same days.

Irvin and Judas exchanged glances, trying to come up with a way to get out of the situation. In an attempt to escape, they started making up stories to persuade her. Unfortunately, she responded with a sarcastic laugh. Other staff members, overhearing the conversation, also began to scold Irvin and Judas, neglecting their own tasks. This gave her even more momentum, and she started to berate them further. Finally, she issued a stern warning and told them to leave the staff room. Irvin and Judas told Vimal about the incident, and Vimal burst out laughing, unable to stop. Vimal said, "Thankfully, she forgot to notice me." In response, Irvin and Judas start to profanities him in unison.

Even though she had warned Irvin and Judas, they listened but still refused to stop skipping classes. During their first year, they had a lot of free periods. When a class was free, the students were expected to stay outside until the next session began, with each period lasting 50 minutes. One day, during a free period, Irvin, Judas, and Vimal decided to go out for milkshakes. As they were heading toward the two-wheeler parking lot, two of their classmates, Niyaz and John, approached them and asked, "Where are you guys going? Mind if we join?" Initially, Irvin hesitated but eventually agreed to let them tag along.

They started their bikes, and the five of them rode to the milkshake shop and enjoyed their drinks. This marked the beginning of Irvin's efforts to socialize with others. At the end of their outing, the group took a selfie and then returned to college. Within a few days, Niyaz grew close to Irvin, Judas, and Vimal, and they became best friends. Irvin also had a habit of introducing his closest friends, Rashed Khan and Jeya Krishnan, to his new friends.

Vimal and Judas had already become friends with Rashed Khan and Jeya Krishnan. Irvin, Judas, Niyaz, and Vimal formed a group on WhatsApp, naming it the Planning Committee. They used the group to plan and organize their outings. For their first trip, Niyaz arranged a visit to the Green Hills, which were approximately ninety-three kilometers away. This was their first excursion together, and for Irvin, it was his first-ever bike ride on a hillside.

During the trip, Irvin introduced his best friend, Jeya Krishnan, to Niyaz. Everything went smoothly until they reached the Green Hills. At the first bend, Niyaz and Jeya Krishnan were waiting. As Irvin was new to riding bikes on hills, he lost control and crashed into Jeya Krishnan's and Judas's bikes, which were parked at the edge. Due to their height, Jeya Krishnan and Niyaz struggled to lift both the Royal Enfield and the Pulsar simultaneously but were unable to manage the weight.

Niyaz exclaimed, "Ada gommala!" and fell onto the curb, while Irvin tumbled onto the road. After a few minutes, everyone exchanged profanities, sat on the road, and burst into laughter. After thirty minutes, they resumed their journey, took pictures, explored the area, and eventually returned home.

Chapter XXVI

Navigating New Horizons

Tales of Transformation and Connection

Irvin, Judas, Niyaz, and Vimal started hanging out together. After gaining Niyaz's friendship, Irvin, Judas, and Vimal found it easier to connect with other students, except for the girls. For the past five years, Irvin hadn't spoken to any girls; in fact, he had forgotten how to talk to them and was now afraid to do so. Despite this fear, he couldn't help but notice the most beautiful girl in his class. She was slim, fair-skinned, and undeniably beautiful, and her name was Rose.

Initially, Irvin was merely attracted to her, but after a few days, that attraction grew into a crush. He would watch her in class, and especially after college when she walked to the bus stop. Irvin would rush to get his bike along with Vimal, making attempts to grab her attention with playful taunts. Unfortunately, these attempts failed. After a few days, Irvin noticed that one of his classmates was getting close to her, and his friends began teasing him about it.

This infuriated Irvin. Due to the large number of students in his class, he hadn't learned most of their names, so he asked about the guy who was close to Rose. Vimal replied, "His name is Vamsi." Now that Irvin knew his name, he wanted to confront him. After returning home, Irvin recounted the events to Paraman. Paraman advised him, "Brother, we can fight with others over any problem, but we never fight over women. That's the mark of a true man."

Typically, Irvin would follow Paraman's advice after his parents'. These words resonated deeply with him, so he abandoned his plan to confront Vamsi over Rose. Time passed quickly, and Irvin eventually discovered that Rose was already in a relationship with someone else and that Vamsi was just a friend. Upon hearing this, Irvin stopped fantasizing about her and put an end to his feelings. With that chapter closed, Irvin, Judas, and Vimal began socializing with other students.

On February 14, Valentine's Day, the college observes two distinct dress codes: those who oppose love wear black, while those who are in love or support love wear white. Niyaz and his friends are instructed to wear black. Altogether, 20 people in black attire headed out to watch a movie.

During this time, Irvin met another classmate who soon became his close friend, Yogi. Later, Yogi joined the Planning Committee. A few weeks later, Irvin learned that Yogi was also from Kettapettai and had studied with Phoebe until the third grade. To Irvin's surprise, he also discovered that Yogi had been his classmate in Lower and Upper Kindergarten.

Irvin recognized some of the faces from his time in Lower Kindergarten, but he couldn't recall Yogi's face. Nonetheless, Irvin and Yogi found themselves on a shared journey once again. After seven months, Irvin, Judas, and Vimal successfully formed friendships with most of their classmates, except for the girls, Venkat, and his friends. However, Irvin did have a few conversations with Sujith, Udhaya, John, and others.

Now that college had become interesting for Irvin, he stopped taking unnecessary leaves and kept his attendance in good standing. The class teacher was surprised and encouraged him to keep it up. The other subject teachers, who had barely noticed Irvin before, would sometimes ask, "Do you belong to this class? I've never seen you in my lectures." Despite this, everything went smoothly, and Irvin even managed to score good marks in his semester exams.

One day, the Tamil Nadu government announced the closure of all colleges and schools, instructing everyone to stay indoors due to the outbreak of COVID-19. The virus claimed many lives, including those of celebrities, while others came close to death but managed to survive. During this challenging time, the college administration decided to continue classes through Google Meet, and the teachers asked students to submit their assignments via Google Classroom.

The entire world had transformed into a different reality. Previously, the college management had enforced a rule: "No mobile phones in the classroom." Now, students were required to attend classes using their mobile phones via Google Classroom. The world faced one of the greatest tragedies in history. Maanya's youngest sister, a nurse, contracted COVID-19, and the virus also spread to her daughters, Hartley and Bathsheba. Many businessmen, vegetable vendors, and auto drivers experienced severe poverty during this period.

On the other hand, Irvin was content with his Kettapettai friends. He attended classes on his mobile phone, kept the audio muted, and spent time with his buddies. Fortunately, Rajan, being a retired government employee, managed to support the family during the pandemic. This continued for two whole years. In the first year, the government mandated that all students pass, including those with exam arrears. Irvin easily passed the first year and was promoted to the second year. During the second year, Irvin attended classes entirely online.

In the planning committee, Irvin, Judas, Niyaz, Vimal, and Yogi gathered either at Judas's house or Irvin's house to study for exams. Thanks to the open-book format and the use of Google, the students achieved excellent marks. Irvin successfully completed his second year and advanced to the final year.

Chapter XXVII

Resurgence of Irvin

Navigating Loss, Love, and New Beginnings.

During the two-year COVID-19 pandemic in India, the first year saw a rapid surge in cases, leaving the world struggling to find a cure. In response, the Indian government imposed a strict lockdown to curb the spread of the virus. During this period, Irvin remained mostly confined to his home, indulging in good food, which led to significant weight gain.

Occasionally, his friends from Kettapettai would gather on Irvin's veranda, sitting on the compound wall to chat. The second wave of the virus proved to be even more devastating. However, by this time, the World Health Organization (WHO) had introduced a treatment for COVID-19, prompting the government to ease restrictions while maintaining certain regulations.

In the third year, students were required to complete team projects, leading them to request temporary full-day attendance at college. During this brief period, Irvin made a strong impression on both his class teacher and subject instructors. He dedicated himself to preparing the project materials with great effort.

However, Irvin, Judas, and Vimal distanced themselves from Niyaz due to his domineering nature, which prompted them to form closer bonds with other classmates. Overall, everything went smoothly. One day, Irvin received a call from Vamsi, who said, "Udhaya is dead; he committed suicide." Irvin was stunned. Within a few hours, all the boys from the class gathered at Udhaya's home.

Those who were close to him mourned his loss, while others put on a display of grief to maintain their image. Irvin felt sorrowful and began to observe those around him. He noticed Venkat, who was struggling to breathe from the weight of his grief—Venkat had been Udhaya's only close friend. During this time, Rajan's sister had completed the construction of a new house in the Nandhamal district, so Rajan and Maanya decided to attend the housewarming ceremony with their family. Maanya insisted that Irvin join them for the event.

Irvin was conflicted, uncertain whether he should attend the housewarming with his family or stay at the funeral with his classmates. After a few moments of deliberation, Irvin decided to attend the funeral, defying Maanya's wishes. The following day, the college faculty and female classmates arrived, shedding tears and expressing their sorrow.

While everyone mourned, Venkat struggled the most to come to terms with the loss of his best friend. During this difficult time, Vamsi and his family supported Venkat, who was so overwhelmed with grief that he couldn't eat or sleep. Irvin and his classmates banded together to encourage him to eat. The students of III B.A. deeply missed Udhaya. Even the hardships of COVID-19 hadn't caused them such heartbreak, but Udhaya's death left a profound and lasting scar on their hearts, like a tattoo.

After Udhaya's death, the III B.A. class remained silent for two days. The professors entered the classroom and were struck by the students' dark, pale expressions. Unable to proceed with their lessons, they left the classroom and returned to their respective offices. Every staff member made a special effort to support Irvin's class representative and Udhaya's best friend, Venkat. After this tragedy, life gradually returned to normal for Irvin and his classmates.

During this time, Irvin rekindled his relationship with Phoebe. He began to socialize more with his female classmates and even made his first close female friend, Sowthriya. After enduring the greatest storm, the field of life began to flourish, ready for a new harvest. Irvin, Judas, and Vimal successfully completed their undergraduate studies.

After earning his B.A. in English, Rajan and Maanya decided that Irvin should continue his education and pursue a Master's degree, so he reapplied to Benjamin Herbert College. Vimal made the same decision, but his family preferred that he secure a seat in an aided (government) institution. Judas, seeking a change, applied to the same college but opted for a Master's in Social Work. Irvin's puppy love with Phoebe was now fully revived, and they began dating.

Chapter XXVIII

Redefining Destiny

Irvin's Leap into a New Chapter.

During the lockdown, Irvin grew bored and began exploring his messenger app. He navigated to his blocked contacts and came across Phoebe's contact. Irvin thought to himself, "There's no connection between us anymore, so there's no reason to keep her blocked." He decided to unblock her. Twenty-four hours later, Irvin posted a status update, which Phoebe noticed. She responded, "Why did you unblock my number?" That was all it took—soon, Irvin and Phoebe were talking like they used to. After a month, Irvin found himself falling in love with Phoebe all over again.

One day, Irvin finally proposed to Phoebe. She was thrilled and loved the way Irvin expressed his feelings, but because he hadn't explained why he broke up with her before, she felt uncertain about accepting his proposal. At the same time, she couldn't bring herself to reject it outright.

Because of Irvin's past mistake, Phoebe made him wait for her answer, just as she had in the past. However, this time, Irvin lost his patience and asked her to make up her mind about whether she reciprocated his love or not. After more than five hours of consideration, Phoebe finally accepted his proposal.

Initially, they nurtured their relationship through chatting. Gradually, they moved on to video calls, and eventually, they started going out on dates. Most of the time, Phoebe was the one who paid the bills. Phoebe came from a sophisticated family, while Irvin came from a middle-class background, so Rajan gave him some money to cover petrol expenses.

Despite this, Phoebe insisted on paying the bills herself. Irvin and Phoebe were much happier than before, having grown more mature, which allowed them to understand each other better. Though Irvin was short-tempered, he would always apologize when he made a mistake. Truthfully, he was usually the one at fault.

Irvin was confident that he would secure a seat at his college. However, Maanya was concerned that they might need to rely on Vimal's parents for help again. Fortunately, Irvin received a message from the college informing him that he had been admitted to the first shift of the PG program. Twenty minutes later, Yogi called Irvin to let him know that he, too, had been admitted to the same class, as Tabitha, who had become their friend the previous year. Judas also received a message from the college, inviting him for an interview. A week later, Judas passed the interview and secured an aided seat.

However, he was torn between choosing English or Social Work as his major. He took a week to gather information about the prospects of Social Work. Meanwhile, Irvin and Yogi tried to persuade him to join the English program. After a week of deliberation, Judas decided to go for Social Work and opted to join the English program instead. He went to the college, convinced the professor, and through their influence, secured admission in the second shift.

This meant that Irvin and Judas would now be studying at the same college and in the same major. A few days later, Phoebe left for Chandras District to continue her studies, putting a distance of 320 kilometers between them. Meanwhile, Irvin successfully began his postgraduate studies.

Initially, he struggled to wake up early in the morning and arrive at college on time, as he had been accustomed to the evening shift during his undergraduate years and felt more comfortable with that schedule. While Irvin quickly bonded with his male classmates, he once again experienced anxiety when it came to talking to girls.

When Irvin came home from college, he would have lunch and then go straight to bed because he was exhausted. However, every sixth hour, Judas would call him to share everything that had happened in his class. These calls disrupted Irvin's sleep. Although Irvin disliked having his rest interrupted, he put up with it for the sake of their friendship. Meanwhile, Yogi began spending more time with his female friends, leaving Irvin alone.

At first, Irvin tried to control his frustration, but after a while, he could no longer tolerate Yogi's actions. Irvin had never been accustomed to being alone in any situation, so it felt strange and uncomfortable for him. Additionally, he had never really liked his class, which only added to his feelings of isolation.

One day, Irvin confided in Judas about Yogi's behavior and his dissatisfaction with his new class. Judas suggested that Irvin join his class instead. Initially, Maanya didn't approve of Irvin's request to switch classes, but after a few days, when Irvin asked again, she took her time and eventually agreed. Irvin then asked Venkat for advice on how to write a letter to request a change in his stream. After getting some suggestions, Irvin drafted the letter. Before making the switch, he spoke to Tabitha, encouraging her to change streams with him since she also wasn't happy with her class.

The next day, Irvin went straight to the HOD's office, presented his case with some fabricated reasons, and, despite knowing they were false, the HOD approved his request. She even offered him some tips on how to persuade the Vice Principal. During the break, Irvin said goodbye to his new friends. Later, Vimal and Irvin waited outside the Vice Principal's office with the letter in hand, ready to make the change.

At that time, many students were waiting outside the principal's office to get admitted to the college. Irvin overheard that a girl had just been admitted to the MA English evening stream. Afterwards, Irvin went to the Vice Principal's office, where the Vice Principal reviewed and signed his letter in green ink. Now, Irvin was pleased to be reunited with his old friends—Judas, Venkat, and

Sowthriya—as well as some other unfamiliar classmates from the previous year.

Chapter XXIX

Navigating New Paths

The Evening Class Saga

At Benjamin Herbert College, the teachers and staff tend to value the morning shift students more than those in the evening shift. Even in the IT department, the staff questioned Irvin, saying, "Why are you switching from the morning to the evening shift?" However, Irvin was determined to escape his current class, so he decided to make the change. He successfully switched his stream and went home. The next day, Irvin wondered how he would make friends in his new class, having joined the evening shift a month late. That afternoon, he attended his first day in the evening shift.

In this shift, the total class strength was thirty-six students, with only eight boys and twenty-eight girls. Irvin chose to sit on the last bench with Judas, Venkat, and Puneeth. He was particularly curious about the girl who rode a heavyweight motorcycle, a Royal Enfield.

Before joining the evening class, Judas called Irvin and said, "Dude, a girl joined our stream today, and she rides a Royal Enfield, bro." Imagining her to be stocky and strong, Irvin talked about this girl to Phoebe. On his first day in the evening class, Irvin asked Judas, "Where is she, bro?" Judas responded, "Who, bro?" Irvin clarified, "The one who rides the Royal Enfield." Judas then pointed her out. Irvin was stunned when he saw her—she was slender and looked like the perfect girl, completely different from what he had imagined.

According to Irvin, most girls rode lightweight motorcycles like scooters or four-speed engines such as Splendors. This led him to assume that the girl riding the Royal Enfield must be heavyset, but he was wrong. On the same day, she had a misunderstanding with her classmate Silas and harshly scolded him. Irvin thought to himself, "She must be an arrogant girl; we'll have to be careful around her." He asked Judas for her name, and Judas replied, "Her name is Bamini."

For the next two weeks, Irvin only spoke to his old classmates before heading home. However, one day, he noticed that one of the girls in his class kept glancing at him frequently. This puzzled him, especially since she seemed to be quite talkative.

Irvin decided to break the ice with his new classmates, starting with the girl who had been frequently glancing at him. He soon learned that she had previously studied at the college on the morning shift, and her name was Aadhiya. Meanwhile, Bamini discovered that Irvin was fond of the Japanese language through his WhatsApp username, as she was also familiar with Japanese. Irvin enjoyed keeping those around him happy and often used humor to lighten the mood. His jokes, though sometimes containing adult humor, brought laughter to his classmates. Both Bamini and Aadhiya grew to like Irvin because of his cheerful and humorous personality.

Recently, Irvin discovered that Bamini was from his hometown, which excited him. He talked about her with his family and even mentioned her to Phoebe because Bamini resembled Phoebe. Bamini and Aadhiya would often say to Irvin, "She's absent today. If she were here, she would burst into laughter that none of us could control.

"Despite their attempts to describe her appearance, Irvin couldn't recall who they were talking about. Two days later, Bamini and Aadhiya introduced Irvin to the girl who couldn't control her laughter—her name was Sandra. Suddenly, Irvin remembered something. Before joining the evening shift, Judas had shared details about his first day of college and mentioned a conversation with Puneeth where he said, "All the girls are unattractive except Sandra and Padma." Judas had also hyped up Sandra to Irvin. Now, in the present, Irvin finally saw her.

In Irvin's first class, he noticed her, and she was the only one wearing a thick thread with a gold pendant. Irvin felt sorry for her, assuming she came from a poor family. Around the same time, the English department organized a program called Confluence. In Confluence, students from the English department could participate in various competitions and compete for medals and the overall championship.

Typically, Irvin preferred motivating participants rather than participating himself. Judas and his other classmates were participating in Confluence, so they had to come in the morning for practice and attend regular classes in the afternoon. After three days, Judas asked to join them, even though he wasn't participating in any competitions.

During this time, Irvin became more familiar with Aadhiya, Bamini, Karl, and Sandra. During the practice sessions, Irvin offered some tips for their drama. During a break, the group discussed the scriptwriter for their drama, who needed to arrive early so the cast could rehearse their lines. Everyone was waiting for her arrival, and Irvin was especially eager to meet her.

After thirty minutes, she arrived, handed them the script, and left. This was the first time Irvin had seen her, so he asked Judas about her. Judas replied, "Her name is Jemimah." Irvin thought she seemed intelligent. Now, Irvin was familiar with everyone in his class. During this period, Irvin befriended Aadhiya, Bamini, Jemimah, Judas, Karl, Puneeth, Sandra, and Venkat.

Gradually, these friendships began to feel like family. Bamini would call all the boys "Anna" (meaning "brother"), and Aadhiya also called Irvin "Anna" because his annoying habits reminded her of her brother. Irvin was now experiencing a new kind of friendship circle that he had never had before.

Chapter XXX

Unspoken Wounds

The Path to Reconciliation

The practice sessions have concluded, and now Aadhiya, Bamini, Judas, Sandra, and Venkat are ready to take the stage. Irvin, as the photographer, is excelling at his role, while the others are managing costumes and offering various forms of support. The day was a success, and it also happened to be Judas' birthday. To celebrate, he decided to treat all his friends. After the event, everyone, except Jemimah, attended the celebration. Since Jemimah is a hosteller, the college required her to have a permission letter, preventing her from joining.

Everyone arrived at the restaurant and placed their orders. However, after several minutes, not a single dish had been served. Frustrated, Sandra urged Irvin to speak with the staff. Judas observed her reaction. After the meal, Judas repeatedly asked Sandra, "How was the treat? Were you satisfied with it?" His persistent questioning made her feel uncomfortable, so she decided to avoid speaking with him for a while.

Judas typically confided all his feelings in Irvin, so he admitted, "Bro, I don't know what I did wrong. She's refusing to talk to me. "Irvin responded, "Relax, bro. don't rush things; just be patient. She'll come around." However, Irvin privately wondered, "Why is he so fixated on this?" and eventually asked Judas directly. At first, Judas tried to change the subject and avoided giving a clear answer. This unresolved issue led Judas to fall into depression.

One day, as usual, Judas called Irvin, but Irvin immediately noticed that his tone was slurred as if he were intoxicated. Irvin asked, "Dude, are you drunk?" Judas replied, "Yes." Once again, Judas began complaining about Sandra's actions. Frustrated, Irvin, feeling tense, asked, "Are you in love with Sandra?" At first, Judas gave evasive answers, but Irvin pressed him for the truth. Eventually, Judas admitted that he had indeed fallen in love with Sandra.

Irvin asked, "When did this happen?" Judas replied, "I liked her from the moment I first saw her. I also learned about her through some distant relatives, so I found her Instagram account and went through all her reels and posts." After listening to Judas' confession, Irvin decided to confront Sandra about the situation, but Judas objected to the idea.

Sandra completely ghosted Judas for a while. He waited for some time before trying to approach her again, but eventually, he gave up. Despite Irvin's attempts to persuade him otherwise, Judas was adamant about moving on. However, a few days later, Judas set his sights on another girl, the intellectual Jemimah. Meanwhile, Irvin had undergone a major transformation. Previously, he never interacted with or even looked at girls, but now he had them bursting into laughter with his humorous expressions and witty jokes.

After the first semester, Irvin and Sandra unknowingly grew close. They enjoyed sharing personal matters with each other. One day, Sandra confided in Irvin that she felt left out because Aadhiya and Bamini had become close friends and she felt alone. At first, Irvin wasn't sure how to respond, but eventually, he managed to comfort her. On alternating days, Irvin and his friends attended their diploma courses. After two weeks, Irvin became upset with Sandra because, although she had been engaging well with him in the morning, he later felt ignored by her.

Irvin decided to stop talking to Sandra. Even when she approached him, he would give irrelevant or one-word answers to avoid her. From his behavior, Sandra realized that Irvin was upset with her, though she didn't know why. The next day, Sandra's face looked unusually dull, which was out of character for her. Judas urged him, "Bro, she looks pale because of you. You should talk to her." Irvin refused. Though he also noticed her change, his heart urged him to ask what was wrong, but his resentful mind told him to ignore her. This marked the first conflict between Irvin and Sandra.

On the other hand, Jemimah was distancing herself from Irvin's group. She struggled with an inferiority complex, feeling that Irvin, Judas, Puneeth, and Venkat had been friends for a long time and wouldn't fully accept her as one of their own. She was also saddened by being separated from her best friend. Sowthriya had stopped talking to Irvin, Judas, and Venkat, only interacting with Sandra.

Irvin eventually noticed all of this. He didn't like seeing his group become divided. He thought to himself, "This is my family, but now there's a crack in it. If I ignore this, the whole thing will fall apart. I need to fix this quickly." Irvin took the first step and began investigating to resolve the issue. He started by speaking with Aadhiya and Bamini, but they were just as confused as he was. After returning home, Irvin called Aadhiya and Bamini, explaining that Sandra had already confided in him about the situation.

He then reached out to Jemimah and listened to her concerns. Irvin responded, "Judas and I have been friends for a while, and Venkat and Puneeth were classmates before. We only became a group this year. So, like you, there are others who joined us recently." Irvin contacted everyone except Sowthriya and Sandra, managing to clear up most of the misunderstandings.

The next day, Irvin tried to speak with Sowthriya, but she avoided him and left with Sandra. After college ended, Irvin waited at the bus stop to talk to Sowthriya. When she arrived with Sandra, he asked her about her issue, believing he could help resolve it. Irvin then tried to leave the area.

Suddenly, a feminine voice called out to him from behind. "Don't go. Turn around." Irvin recognized it was Sandra and turned to face her but avoided making eye contact. She insisted that he talk to her and look her in the eye, but Irvin struggled to do so. He promised to reach out to her later in the evening to address the issue.

As he had promised, Irvin contacted Sandra, and she inquired about why he had been avoiding her. Irvin explained his reasons for ghosting her. Sandra revealed that she had already learned about this from Venkat, who had described it as "she is using me." This phrase deeply hurt her, and she cried extensively.

She shared her feelings with her close friend, Paru, who offered her comfort. While discussing the issue, Sandra said, "I don't care about what others have done to me, but when you did this, I couldn't endure it, and I cried a lot." Irvin understood the issue and said, "What Venkat said is true, but I swear I never used the phrase 'she's using me.'

There was a misunderstanding." In the end, Irvin and Sandra reconciled. Irvin deeply admired Sandra, and from that day forward, he resolved, "No matter what happens, I will never abandon her." Meanwhile, the others reconciled and were reunited as a group, as Irvin had hoped, except for Sowthriya.

Chapter XXXI

Navigating the Storm

Irvin's Pain and Friendship.

Everything has gone well for Irvin. He has great friends like Aadhiya, Bamini, Judas, Jemimah, Karl, Sandra, Puneeth, and Venkat. I paved the way for Irvin, and he made the most of it. I provided him with opportunities to experience a new environment and learn important lessons. I admire Irvin for his determination and dedication, but I disapprove of his impatience and quick temper. These flaws have caused him to lose some valuable people in his life.

In his second semester, Irvin's academic life was filled with joy, but he faced overwhelming pressure from his romantic relationship that he struggled to manage. Irvin and Phoebe shared some beautiful moments together, but he also exhibited certain flaws, such as unconsciously displaying male superiority.

During their arguments, his impulsive temper led him to utter harsh words that wounded her gentle heart.

Despite these challenges, their love for each other remained strong, and overall, his romantic life progressed smoothly.

One day, Phoebe shared a conversation she had with her mother. Her mother had said, "I want you to marry someone from our caste and status; his religion doesn't matter to me." Phoebe knew very well that Irvin despised caste-based thinking. These words lingered in his mind, and after some time, they ignited a major argument, ultimately laying the groundwork for their separation. This parting, though reached through mutual understanding, reduced their long-term relationship to ashes.

Even though Irvin had shown his harsh side to Phoebe during their argument, I saw him—he was shattered into a million pieces. Rajan and Maanya were quick to notice the sadness on their son's face. Irvin found himself torn, struggling between the weight of family expectations and his love for Phoebe. Wanting to release his overwhelming sorrow without his parents' awareness, he retreated to the bathroom, turned on the tap, and broke down in tears.

Everyone in Kettapettai offered their advice: "If you want her, you'll have to either elope or let her go. Choose wisely." His best friend, Judas, gave suggestions from different perspectives. While some thoughtless individuals turn to alcohol to drown their pain, Irvin was of a different nature; he steadfastly refuses to take that path.

Now, Irvin is unsure how to cope with his suffering. His friends from Kettapettai used to be a source of comfort during tough times, but now they have grown up and are focused on their own lives and families. When news of his breakup reached his college friends, some pitied him, while others judged him for the separation.

However, only one person truly supported him—the kind-hearted Sandra. Typically, she wouldn't reach out to anyone unless she needed help, so it was usually Irvin who contacted her. But this time, she called him, checked on him, lifted his spirits with her clever humor, and made him laugh. She even video-called him, observed his expressions, and soothed him with her words.

This was exactly what Irvin had hoped for from his friends, but they failed to provide it. However, Sandra became the remedy for his mental anguish. Irvin, who already had a short temper, found himself at the height of his frustration during this period. One day, a misunderstanding occurred between him and Vimal, and Irvin was waiting for the right moment to confront him.

That moment came when they were all at a restaurant, and Vimal arrived, greeting everyone. In his unstable state of mind, Irvin impulsively lashed out at Vimal with harsh words in front of everyone. While Irvin was fuming, Sandra handed him her food and drink to help calm him down. Not only did Irvin appreciate her actions, but I did as well. I admired the way she cared for him and her genuine kindness.

Aadhiya and Bamini also supported Irvin and tried to distract him from his sadness, but Sandra helped him in a way that was truly unique. Thanks to her, Irvin managed to recover from his emotional breakdown within a few weeks. Without her, he would have struggled to overcome his grief, like a child trying to stand on unsteady feet.

After he regained his composure, Irvin developed a deep respect for Sandra and felt profoundly grateful to have her as a friend. Irvin had always been appreciative of his friends who had supported him during difficult times, and he knew he would remain thankful to Sandra for the rest of his life.

Personally, I dislike his negative traits. From this point onward, I have prepared and woven a special thread into his life journey, so stay tuned.

Chapter XXXII

The Breaking Point

Irvin's Struggle with Friendship and Trust.

Every mortal experiences defining phrases or unforgettable moments in their lifetime. Similarly, Irvin navigated a range of emotions throughout his journey, but it was his time in postgraduate studies that he considered the "most valuable and memorable period of his life." During his first year, Irvin was filled with joy, thanks to the company of his friends Aadhiya, Bamini, Jemimah, Khanika, Sujith, Sandra, Vamsi, and Venkat.

Even though Irvin endured heartache, these wonderful people helped him forget his pain, especially Sandra, who went a step further in supporting him. During this period, Irvin and Sandra often clashed due to misunderstandings. However, after a few days, they reached an understanding and continued their relationship.

In his first year, Irvin formed friendships with Julia, Khanika, and Sujith. Julia, who had once been his classmate and someone he disliked intensely, became a close friend after they truly got to know each other. Irvin had adopted a principle from his Kettapettai friends: "If a friend is struggling through tough times, we must help them at any cost; if not, we should cut ties with them."

Julia struggled due to her toxic relationship, and Irvin, along with Khanika, became her pillar of support. By the end of the first year, Irvin had also formed a friendship with Janet. Everything seemed to be falling into place for him. Meanwhile, Irvin and Sandra developed a deep bond, akin to the legendary friendship of Damon and Pythias. They spoke three times a week, sharing moments and secrets from their pasts.

The rapport between Irvin and Sandra was perfect, with Sandra even admitting that he was "special" to her. Even during the semester holidays, they continued to care for each other. Irvin and his friends successfully completed their first year and were prepared to embark on their final year.

Irvin anticipated that his final year would be the happiest of his life, but I have a particular twist that will shape him into a more reformed individual. At the start of his second year, Irvin and Sandra had another falling out due to a misunderstanding caused by Irvin. In college,

Sandra began giving him less attention, spending most of her time with Judas. This weighed heavily on Irvin's mind, but he hesitated to address it.

Later that evening, Sandra called him, and Irvin, overwhelmed with frustration, lost his temper, leading the conversation to escalate into an argument. In the heat of the moment, he blurted out harsh words: "While you and he are blandishment up, how can I come between you?" These words cut deep into Sandra's heart. Though Irvin didn't mean what he said—he was just using casual, colloquial language—it became a source of immense disappointment for her.

Irvin deeply regretted his actions and sought forgiveness from Sandra, but she was unwilling to forgive and restore their friendship. Judas and Sandra attended church on Sundays, so Irvin asked Judas to deliver his heartfelt apology. However, Judas only partially relayed Irvin's sentiments and omitted his true feelings, which greatly frustrated Irvin.

Additionally, Judas informed Aadhiya that "Irvin dislikes me speaking with Sandra," a notion that Irvin had never considered and did not understand why Judas would make such a claim. After a few weeks, Sandra forgave

Irvin, but their relationship was no longer the same as before.

Irvin sensed that something was amiss, but she refused to disclose what was wrong. For a few days, things were relatively peaceful between them. Irvin had a habit of affectionately rubbing the heads of his sisters, so he did the same for Aadhiya, Bamini, and Sandra.

From the beginning, Sandra felt uncomfortable with this behavior but refused to address it. One day, during a conversation, Irvin gently said, "If you feel uneasy about my actions, please let me know, and I will make sure not to repeat them." However, her response was harsh and unacceptable to him, leading to a major fallout between them. As a result, they stopped communicating.

Meanwhile, Judas frequently rubbed Sandra's hand, which was bothersome to Irvin. This behavior pushed Irvin to his breaking point. He confronted Judas, demanding that he stop touching Sandra's hand. Judas responded, "If you want to rub someone's hand, then rub Jemimah's hand. I didn't touch Sandra's hand." This reply only intensified Irvin's anger. On another front, Janet, who initially acted as a mediator between Irvin and Sandra, had recently become less effective in her role. Irvin found himself overwhelmed and struggled to find solutions during this period.

Chapter XXXIII

The Conspiracy & Echoes of Trust and Conflict

Every mortal makes mistakes. Some rectify them, while others remain unaware they've even erred. In Irvin's life, he made many mistakes, but over time, he recognized them and transformed into a better person. During this period, Irvin often used Janet as a mediator between him and Sandra. Whenever Irvin and Sandra had a disagreement, he would ask Janet to intervene on his behalf. However, Sandra disapproved of this approach. She preferred to keep their issues private. Irvin, eager to resolve conflicts quickly, sought Janet's assistance despite Sandra's wishes.

On the other hand, Irvin's anger gradually turned into resentment toward Judas. You might wonder, "Why did Irvin harbor such deep animosity toward Judas?" To answer that, we must revisit the past. When Irvin and Sandra grew close, Judas assumed Irvin had developed romantic feelings for her. He persistently urged Irvin to pursue a relationship with Sandra, something that greatly displeased Irvin.

Initially, Irvin told Judas to stop this nonsense, but Judas paid no heed to his words. During Irvin's conflict with Phoebe, Judas advises him, "Forget about Phoebe and marry Sandra. I'll support you both, and I'll even speak to your mother when the time comes." Judas subtly planted the idea in Irvin's mind. After Irvin's separation from Phoebe, Judas continued bringing up the idea of him pursuing Sandra. During this time, however, Irvin unexpectedly grew close to Jemimah, becoming good friends with her.

Now, Judas twisted Irvin's feelings, saying, "So, you love both Jemimah and Sandra? Who's your wife, bro? Or are you going to choose two wives?" These words infuriated Irvin, who scolded him harshly. However, Judas continued this talk for a long time until Irvin eventually stopped speaking to him altogether. Irvin believed Judas was getting possessive whenever he saw him talking to Jemimah, so to avoid further comments, he began distancing himself from her.

Irvin did this for the sake of his friendship, but Judas continued his manipulative behavior, true to the meaning of his name. During Irvin and Sandra's separation,

Aadhiya, Bamini, and Venkat believed Irvin's actions stemmed from possessiveness.

His unstable and impulsive behavior gave that impression. Unable to find a solution, Irvin made irrational decisions that ultimately led to a tragic failure, causing Sandra to resent him. However, Irvin's confrontation with Judas was not born out of possessiveness, but rather due to an ugly act Judas committed, something no one else knew about.

Irvin didn't know how to approach Sandra to resolve the issue. Once again, he made the same mistake by sending Julia as a messenger. Julia hesitated at first, knowing that in the past, Sandra had stopped speaking to her, and their relationship had turned to hatred. She advised Irvin that this was a bad idea.

However, Irvin insisted, asking her to speak to Janet instead, with the condition, "Sandra mustn't know this message is from you. Replace my name with Vimal's." Reluctantly, Janet agreed to the plan.

Janet eventually revealed the truth, telling Sandra that the message had come from Julia. This enraged Sandra, and she decided she never wanted to speak to Irvin again. The person she once cherished had now become someone she despised. All of this was hidden from Irvin, but he sensed that something was wrong between them and resolved to fix it. During this time, Irvin deeply missed the days he had shared with Sandra. After Phoebe, it was Sandra that brought him to tears. Irvin appeared almost unhinged during this period, while Judas, on the other hand, and was pleased with his growing friendship with Sandra.

Before Irvin and Sandra's separation, Irvin confided in Janet that he had bought a customized necklace for Sandra's birthday. Along with this gift, he intended to express that he had developed an infatuation for her (the seed planted by Judas). However, Janet misunderstood the word "infatuation," interpreting it as if Irvin were deeply in love with Sandra. Without Irvin's knowledge, she conveyed this to Sandra. Unsure of how to respond, Sandra turned to her brother for advice.

Irvin lost his patience and made every effort to reach Janet. He was determined to explain everything to Sandra. This wasn't the first time Judas had acted this way. During the COVID-19 pandemic, Judas had desired his best friend's lover. Aware that their relationship wasn't strong at the time, he began subtly laying the groundwork to build a connection with her. During open-book exams, instead of focusing on his test, he spent time texting her on Snapchat. Vimal and I witnessed this first hand. Only Irvin and Vimal truly understood Judas' character, and Irvin wanted to protect Sandra from him. However, instead of asking Irvin why he was doing this, everyone saw him as a troublemaker.

After hearing this, Janet relayed Irvin's plan to Judas and Karl, advising, "Before Irvin tells her, you should confess to her yourself." Judas took their advice and confessed to Sandra, saying, "At first, I had feelings for you, but over time, those feelings faded. Now, I've always seen you as a sister and even as a daughter." Sandra accepted his explanation. This was the same Judas who had once said, "She's using him. I'm not her servant," yet now the same mouth spoke of "sister and daughter."

During this period of separation, Jemimah and Venkat supported Irvin and guided him towards the right path. In the fourth month, Janet was involved in an accident and had to stay at home. Irvin was determined to resolve the issue and earnestly requested a ten-minute conversation with Sandra. She agreed to meet with him. During their discussion, they discovered that Janet had deceived them both. Additionally, Judas, Karl, Janet, and Sandra held a round table meeting where they manipulated Sandra against Irvin. Karl advised, "Now that you know the truth about Irvin, you should stop communicating with him."

Upon hearing this, Irvin became furious with Karl and said, "How dare he speak about me like that? He doesn't respect me or my views. Especially regarding my reasons, he doesn't even consider them." They both reflected on their actions and realized their mistakes. Irvin was now content and hoped to restore their previous relationship. However, Sandra remained unable to move past the situation and continued to distance herself from him. Consequently, Irvin also kept his distance. Irvin completed his third semester amidst much sorrow, confusion, and betrayal.

At the beginning of the final semester, Sandra attempted to reconnect with Irvin. However, Irvin had lost interest in engaging with her and only answered her questions. Reflecting deeply, Irvin decided to say, "I want you to be like you were in the old days. If that's not possible, then stop talking to me." Sandra agreed to his terms. The following day was Irvin's birthday, and he celebrated it with his friends, including Janet and Sandra.

A few days later, Irvin asked Sandra about the reels she had posted with Judas. He assumed she had asked Judas to take her out. To his surprise, it was actually Judas who had taken her out and made the reel. This revelation enraged Irvin, and he shared some of Judas's remarks with her. Judas had once claimed he was not a chauffeur to pick her up and drop her off, yet now he was engaging in such actions. Sandra was aware of some of these issues but remained ignorant of others. Irvin had never encountered such a puke (contemptible) person in his life and wished never to encounter such individuals again.

Sandra wanted to maintain peace with everyone and leave the college on good terms, so she asked Irvin to remain silent. Out of respect for her request, Irvin kept quiet still now or else he would smash his face and tear him apart with his bare hands. Although they resolved their issues, their relationship remained contentious, with frequent clashes. However, they reached a compromise and managed to coexist despite their ongoing conflicts.

In their final confrontation, Sandra told Irvin, "You were once special to me, but now you are just a friend because your words have hurt me. I forgive you, but I can no longer see you as special." Irvin deeply apologized and provided his explanation. Along with Aadhiya, Bamini, Sandra, Venkat, and Irvin spent their remaining days joyfully.

Chapter XXXIV

Unspoken Bonds

Irvin's Memorable Day.

After Irvin and Sandra reached a compromise, Irvin frequently found himself overanalyzing their relationship, searching for the root causes of their conflicts and potential solutions. It suddenly dawned on him that their arguments always seemed to occur the day before special events, such as college functions. While everyone else relished those moments, Irvin and Sandra would avoid each other entirely. Their most prolonged argument happened just before her birthday, prompting Irvin to plan an early celebration. After all, they had only two months left to complete their degrees before parting ways to pursue their individual aspirations.

Irvin shared his plan with Jeya Krishnan and decided to take Sandra to the historic dam in Thendralpalli. Meanwhile, Maanya prepared mutton curry for the occasion and arranged for a cake to be cut at Irvin's stairway house. Irvin wanted to surprise Sandra. The day prior, Irvin, Jeya Krishnan, his brothers, and Shane inflated a bundle of balloons and decorated the venue.

Throughout his life, Irvin had never been particularly close with any female friends; Sandra was the first. Wanting to understand his strengths and weaknesses, he thought her perspective could help him improve for the future. He called Sandra and expressed his request. She responded, "I can't talk about those things while looking into your eyes." Once again, Irvin urged her to share her thoughts about him. She simply replied, "I'll think about it."

On the other hand, Irvin was hesitant to present his idea to his mother, Maanya, as she was always opposed to anything involving girls. Rajan, however, was indifferent to such matters and readily approved of the plan. Knowing Maanya's disapproval, Irvin provided numerous justifications to persuade her to accept it. For the first time ever, the only girl who would be stepping into his home was Sandra.

The following day, Irvin picked her up, and they headed to the ancient dam. He was eager to hear her feedback from the "survey," but to his surprise, she abruptly refused and simply said, "I won't." Irvin felt disappointed by her response. After two hours, they arrived at Irvin's home, where Shane and Jeya Krishnan were busy setting up the place for the cake-cutting.

Irvin gently blindfolded her with his hands and guided her to his stairway house. Once they arrived, he opened the door and removed his hands. She was overjoyed by the birthday surprise and happily enjoyed the cake and mutton curry. Maanya chatted with her for a while, and Shane brought up a Korean series that Irvin didn't like. After some time, Irvin's father, Rajan, came home and engaged in a lively conversation about her hometown. Irvin was taken aback, as Rajan had never spoken so openly with his school friends or his Kettapettai friends, yet he was unusually friendly with her. Afterwards, Irvin and Sandra returned to his stairway house, where he offered her some advice.

However, his awkward proverb left an unfortunate impression on what was supposed to be a special moment. Later, Irvin regretted it. After their conversation, Sandra said heartfelt goodbyes to his family, and Irvin dropped her off at her hostel. A few days later, the college held a farewell function, and the whole class was filled with deep emotions, especially Irvin's friends. Their bond wasn't just of the heart but of the soul, so the parting caused a lingering heartache that took time to heal. Puneeth created a special farewell video for their class, which moved Bamini, Aadhiya, and Venkat to tears.

As everything fell into place at the last moment, our heroes were now preparing for their final semester examinations, studying hard to improve their scores. For Irvin, the lingering regret of his earlier misstep weighed heavily on his mind. Determined to make things right, he decided to take Sandra out "ONE LAST TIME." Seeking advice, he turned to the expert, Jeya Krishnan, who offered him a brilliant suggestion.

During the study break, Irvin picked her up, and they went to the theater to watch a movie. Sandra truly enjoyed watching movies, which gave him even more happiness. While watching the film, she took a snap and posted it on Snapchat, sharing her location as well.

Judas, also known as "The Puke," sends her a message saying, "Hey girl, are you at the Maha Theater?" Irvin notices the notification and feels a surge of anger but manages to keep it in check. He's determined to spend time with Sandra without any awkward incidents and is very mindful of it. Sandra remarks, "Your best friend just texted me. Did you see that?" Irvin, trying to stay composed, replies, "That's none of my business," and denies seeing it.

After the movie ended, they decided to go to a nice restaurant for a meal. Irvin noticed that his bike was low on petrol and stopped at a gas station. Accidentally, he mentioned, "If we had taken the direct route, we could have reached Sowthriya's house." Sandra decided to visit Sowthriya and asked him to fill up the tank. They traveled a considerable distance to reach her house, where they spoke with her mother, enjoyed some chaat items, went upstairs, and took a few pictures together.

After a while, Irvin and Sandra bid farewell to Sowthriya's family and headed toward their respective places. Suddenly, Sandra expressed a desire to visit Bamini and spend the remaining time with her. Irvin took the route to Bamini's house. They spent a joyful time together, and after a while, Irvin and Sandra said their goodbyes to Bamini and her mother. Irvin then rode back to her hostel. During the journey, Sandra remarked, "I really enjoyed the day. How about you, Irvin?" Although Irvin was thrilled to have spent time with her, he hesitated to express his feelings and simply gave her a thumbs-up. Afterwards, he dropped her off safely and returned home contentedly.

Chapter XXXV

The End…,

Our heroes entered the final phase of their college lives. After completing their last exams, they gathered for one final lunch together. Like Jemimah, some of their classmates left immediately after the exams. Two days later, Sandra prepared to return to her hometown from Thendralpalli. Before she departed, Irvin and Venkat wanted to see everyone's faces one last time. So, they decided to organize "THE FINAL MEETUP" at Venkat's house.

The day finally arrived. Irvin, Aadhiya, Bamini, Khanika, Puneeth, Sandra, and several others gathered at Venkat's house. They pooled their money and ordered chicken biryani, spending the time playing Uno. After everyone finished the biryani, it was time to bid farewell to Sandra and her family. Her parents had sent a car to Venkat's house to pick her up and collect her belongings from the hostel. Irvin and the others rode their bikes to the hostel with her. She hugged each of them and said her LAST goodbye.

After Udhaya's passing, Venkat became deeply attached to everyone in his class. He struggled to cope with their impending separation and cried profusely, as did Bamini and Aadhiya. Irvin, Vamsi, and Venkat spent four days organizing farewells for their classmates. For the first time, Irvin felt a deep sense of heartache due to the separation from his college friends. His Kettapettai friends lived in his neighborhood, so he was used to seeing his school friends regularly on the streets or at the tea shop. But now, he realized he wouldn't be able to see or talk to his college friends as he had before. This was an unfamiliar experience of separation for him.

Bamini was the last to leave Thendralpalli for her hometown. She and her family planned to depart at 6:00 AM, and Venkat and Vamsi arrived promptly. However, for Irvin, this timing felt like the middle of the night, so he missed the chance to bid her farewell. When he woke up later, he realized what had happened and felt saddened by the missed opportunity. Now, the family had parted ways, each beginning to pursue their individual paths in life.

On the other hand, Irvin and Sandra remained in close contact after college. However, after some time, Irvin began to miss Sandra's presence deeply and often found himself reminiscing about their arguments and cherished memories. Initially, he tried to suppress these feelings, but eventually, he couldn't. During this period, Irvin came to appreciate her worth and regretted his past behavior. In the beginning, Irvin had hurt her fragile heart repeatedly, leaving her deeply saddened by his actions.

However, after Irvin used certain words with her, Sandra completely transformed into a different person. She hardened her heart and began to hold Irvin accountable for every mistake, much like a mother disciplining her child to help them grow. Through her cold and seemingly heartless actions, Irvin slowly began to change and eventually became a reformed person. At the time, Irvin didn't understand her behavior, but now he recognized her true worth. During this period, his mental state completely crumbled. He realized how much he needed her and came to the undeniable conclusion that he had fallen in love with Sandra.

He knew she wouldn't accept him because of his past actions, but he still planned to see her. He contacted her and said, "My friends and I are coming to your hometown, and I also want to see you," and she agreed. Irvin and Paraman went to the Universal bus station to inquire about the timings for buses to her hometown. Meanwhile, Irvin lied to his mother and brother, telling them, "We're planning to go to Karl's housewarming party," and Maanya believed him.

During this time, Sujith, Khanika, and Irvin became close friends. Initially, Irvin suggested the idea to Sujith, asking him to stay over at his place so they could catch the early morning bus together. In Kettapettai, Paraman encouraged him to express his feelings to her. Irvin was extremely anxious, as it was the first time he would propose to someone in person and also his first time traveling on the bus alone.

He had two thoughts in mind: first, to confess all his feelings to her, and second, if she accepted him, he would go to Rajan's workplace to confess his love. On May 3, at 9:00 PM, Shane dropped Irvin off at Sujith's place, located near the Universal bus station. Sujith advised him, "Bro, if she doesn't accept you, don't take it personally—it's her loss." On May 4, at 4:30 AM, Irvin woke up, brushed his teeth, and got ready to catch the bus.

By bus, it takes five hours to reach her hometown, but by two-wheeler or car, it only takes three hours. Irvin couldn't ride his bike because Maanya wouldn't allow him to travel long distances, so he took the bus. The journey was uncomfortable, surrounded by unfamiliar and unpleasant strangers, but he endured it all for Sandra.

Finally, he arrived at her place. A few minutes later, she came to see him, spent some time with him, and then they went to the temple. Before he had a chance to propose, Sandra said, "I've decided that from now on, I won't get close to anyone else." Irvin asked, "Even me?" and she replied, "Yes." Irvin was puzzled and wondered, "Why did she make this decision all of a sudden?" His heart began to race, he started to sweat, and without hesitation, he began his speech.

"Sandra, thank you for your support. You've helped me become a better person, and I've only just realized it. Will you be my friend for life?" she responded, "If time permits." Irvin was puzzled by her answer and clarified, "I want us to be friends for a lifetime. Will you marry me?"

Sandra smiled at him and, without hesitation, said, "No." Irvin felt a sense of relief because she had rejected him gently. Afterwards, she persuaded him to take an auto to the bus stand, where he waited for thirty minutes to catch the Thendralpalli bus. During this time, Irvin called Sujith and recounted the entire incident. Sujith replied, "I know, man. You guys don't seem to appreciate made-for-each-other matches. Don't be disheartened. It's her loss for not accepting someone like you."

The bus arrived at the Thendralpalli compartment, and Irvin boarded. While riding, Irvin's phone rang, and he answered it. It was Sandra. She asked, "Did you take the bus to Thendralpalli?" He replied, "Yes." She responded, "Let me know when you get home," and he agreed. They ended the call.

After two hours, Paraman called Irvin and asked, "What happened, brother? Did she accept your proposal?" With a melancholic tone, Irvin replied, "No, brother." Suddenly, Paraman began to curse Sandra, but Irvin said, "Stop that, bro. This is her decision, and we shouldn't interfere. Let's stop criticizing her. I want her to be happy. God bless her." After three and a half hours,

Irvin arrived in Kettapettai. He pulled out his phone and called Sandra. "I've reached Kettapettai," he said. "I'd like to talk to you for a few minutes, please." She agreed. Irvin asked, "It's fine that you turned down my proposal, but I'd like to understand why." She replied, "I have no desire to fall in love with anyone." He responded, "If you ever do decide to fall in love, please consider me as an option." She answered, "Okay," and then ended the call.

As of May 4th, Irvin and Sandra's saga officially came to an end. From my perspective, their relationship grew complicated. Despite being on good terms, they hesitated to express their true feelings to each other. What if Irvin crushed her fragile heart again with his hurtful words? She was afraid to accept him.

But she failed to see how much he had changed since the beginning. Irvin's impatience and short temper contributed to the loss of Sandra. If they had communicated openly, they might still be in touch today. Even now, Irvin holds immense respect for her. Though they are apart, Irvin still…still…still loves her deeply. But who cares? Nobody seems to notice. She has moved on with her life, leaving Irvin behind. I don't know what she did to him, but she has left an ever-lasting ripple of impression on his heart.

Two hundred fifty-two years ago, the poet Samuel Taylor Coleridge found himself in a similar situation. Through his reflection, he wrote, "Ode to Dejection." Irvin is experiencing a comparable situation. I hope Irvin achieves the same level of renown as Samuel Taylor Coleridge. I wish him great success in life and am eager to see whether Irvin and Sandra might reconcile or if someone more suitable will come into Irvin's life. May Jesus Christ and Zeus bless Irvin.

The game is over, only when I say it is over. Hahaha..! (Devilish laughter in unison from the Moirai sisters)…,